The No Teacher Left Behind Club

Scott Milam has been teaching various forms of chemistry courses for thirteen years and currently teaches at Plymouth High School in Michigan. He also writes chemistry parody songs that are poorly performed on YouTube and in 2017 was honored as the Michigan Science Teacher of the Year. His diet and social skills are erratic at best. At the time of the first publishing he has not been fired. But if this book sells a million copies he will do as many activities from the book as he can get away with.

D1176947

The No Teacher Left Behind Club

The true race to the bottom

by
Scott Milam

Table of Contents

Chapter 1 - 1st Day of School   Page 1
Chapter 2 - No Teacher Left Behind   Page 20
Chapter 3 - Breakfast for Lunch   page 38
Chapter 4 - The Meeting   page 59
Chapter 5 - Day of Chaos   page 71
Chapter 6 - Lesson Plans   page 92
Chapter 7 - Chemistry with White Jesus   page 113
Chapter 8 - A Below Average Staff Meeting   page 124
Chapter 9 - The Reprimand   page 133
Chapter 10 - Chemistry Celebration   page 143
Chapter 11 - Interdisciplinary Planning   page 159
Chapter 12 - Professional Development   page 167
Chapter 13 - Staff Meeting   page 183
Chapter 14 - Stability   page 193
Chapter 15 - Spirit Week   page 209
Chapter 16 - Cattle   page 225
Chapter 17 - Central Office   page 234
Chapter 18 - The Return   page 254

Chapter 1 The first day of school

My alarm sounded quietly at 5:21 am. The rest of my family was sleeping. I had been up for seven minutes just waiting for the flashing light to start. I quickly shut off the alarm before quietly getting ready for the first day of school. Not the first day of school with students, but the first day back for teachers. I picked out some comfortable khaki slacks and a loose-fitting blue polo shirt. I drove into work feeling well rested. I lived close enough that I barely had time to find a good song before I arrived at Plymouth High School. This came in handy during the icy cold winters in Michigan. I was one of the first cars to park. There were a couple teachers that arrived absurdly early. It had been a restful summer break. I carried in my computer, my backpack and four 2-liters of pop to get me through the first week with sufficient caffeine.

I underestimated how heavy eight liters would be. As my arms burned, I finally arrived at the office to set things down for a minute and rest before preparing for one last long stretch to my classroom. I opened my classroom door and dragged a couple of bags in with me. I turned on the lights and paused for a moment. It was strange seeing my classroom so clean for once. Most posters were down, papers were put away and most of my bookshelves were stored in a storeroom between my room and the physics classroom next door. My classroom was big and I absolutely loved it. I had a lab on one side and a set of desks on the other side. I had plenty of space and I put that space to good use.

This was my 10th year at Plymouth High School and my 14th year of teaching total. I teach in Michigan which was once the best state to teach in. The pay wasn't the highest in the country, but it was higher than most and the cost of living was low. But for the past twenty years it had gotten a little bit worse every year. Don't get me wrong, Michigan is still a great place to teach. In fact, for me life was good. I had great students, I taught the classes that I loved, the subject that I loved, I had lots of equipment and I had a group of close friends teaching with me. Our staff was fun. We ate lunch together, we would dress up for school spirit days and we even occasionally complained about things. I also had a fair amount of autonomy. I got to try out new creative lessons and I had started a YouTube channel a few years prior that I slowly expanded into slightly profitable. I typically made more money from videos about playing video games but there were a few viewers interested in watching a tall lanky Scott Miles in safety goggles explain how chemistry works to them.

I poured myself a glass of pop and set up my teaching desk. Despite my room being cleaned up, my desk was already messy. But before I could unpack or clean, I had a meeting scheduled in just a few minutes. I started a checklist of things that I needed to get done this week so I didn't end up slammed on Thursday. Before I could add much our biology teacher Mary Chase came in. Mary was short and tended to wear funny science shirts. Her current shirt had a suggestive picture of DNA helicase that said it was going to unzip my genes. "Diane is here, she's just grabbing some coffee," Mary informed me. "Do you want to meet in your room or hers?"

"Her room, definitely," I responded. "Otherwise Diane will just make fun of my room the whole time."

I unplugged my computer and carried it next door. We walked through the supply room which was a complete mess. I think Mary shuddered a little bit when she opened the door and saw the disaster. Diane's room was a lot like mine in layout but everything that Diane used for the entire year was always out. Somehow it wasn't messy. She had physics toys and equipment scattered throughout the room. There were flying pigs hanging from the ceiling, there were ramps on her lab tables and a mannequin of Marie Curie sat in a desk at the back of the classroom. I persistently tried reminding her that Curie was a chemist but Diane knew very well that she had won a Nobel prize in both chemistry and physics. Mary and I set up at student desks near the front of the class.

Diane walked in carrying an oversized coffee mug that was filled to the point where it would spill a little bit as she walked. "Damn it," Diane exclaimed as a little bit of coffee hit her hand. She took a big sip to help mitigate the turbulence. "Hey Mary, hey Scott, how was summer?" she asked us both.

"I'm still on summer," Mary responded with slight amount of saltiness. Mary had been teaching for a while and was going to retire in the next one to seven years but she still seemed to like teaching as

3

much as anyone else. Sometimes I was surprised at how many changes she would make to her lessons this late in her career. The three of us taught a large contingent of the students science, and we often had students move from Mary to me and to Diane in their high school careers. Diane had been working with Mary for a long time. I was the first chemistry teacher that had stayed next to them for an extended period of time so I had gradually joined the group but I could work with them for another fifty years and I would still be the odd one out.

"Summer with young kids is not the break that I want it to be," I added. "I'm looking forward to a break with lots of sleep but I fear it might be a while yet."

"I hear you," Diane said and she offered her coffee cup towards my direction. I met her toast with my glass of pop and we both gulped a bit more caffeine. "Shall we start planning?" Diane asked.

"Yes, let's get rolling," Mary replied.

"All right, keep your genes on," Diane replied and then winked. Mary smirked.

The year before we had arranged for some money to work on a science project between our three sets of classes. We were going to have students design tiny houses that had to show environmental improvements that utilized biology, chemistry and physics. We were going to split our students into groups with each group having students from all three classes. Then the students were going to design a model of a tiny house, make a presentation selling their model and the top two groups were going to

4

have their designs used to actually build two tiny houses. We were all pretty excited about it, especially since we had been awarded some grant money for the model construction and the actual construction.

We worked out a schedule where we would introduce the project at the end of the third marking period, and then we would use two weeks for design and model building so that we could do our final construction before the end of the school year. We put together some potential purchases we would be able to make for groups if they desired the materials. We designed a presentation to show our classes and by then it was nearly time for lunch. We wouldn't be able to make groups until later because too many students would transfer in and out of our classes. We had more to do but our principal, Donna Stephens, had arranged for us to have a couple of release days later in the year to put everything together. It had been a productive morning so we decided to break for lunch.

I went and grabbed Josh Roberts. Josh taught math in the same hallway as us. Josh was very funny and tremendously kind towards his students. He had a patience that you hope a math teacher has. He was big and athletic but also had a big goofy smile so he never came off as intimidating. He also reads a tremendous number of books every year. I joke that he must be grading multiple-choice problems since he has so much time to read. We spent many mornings checking in with each other and talking rather than finish setting up our lessons for the day. Josh and I walked out chatting about a book that Josh had read this summer about cognitive science.

"It's crazy how little we get taught about learning," Josh quipped. "There are basic things I can do differently that have a substantial impact on student learning, but I only happened to come upon these methods via luck."

"You mean you didn't find the professional development last year about data analysis helpful to your teaching?" I asked sarcastically. Josh briefly looked annoyed as he revisited a memory he had nearly forgotten. That presentation had not actually shown any data for our district. It had been an entire presentation with generic data analysis and it was a complete waste of time that looked like it had been thrown together at the last minute. Bad professional development was a theme at our school and we took great pleasure in reminding each other about the worst offenders.

Josh drove an old car, so I had to wait for him to reach across to unlock the door. But his car was clean enough to eat off of. I think he would have let me drive occasionally if my car was not consistently filled with trash and chaos. In spite of the cleanliness he apologized as he moved his sunglasses from my seat. I was tall, but Josh was taller and bigger so I had to scoot my seat forward a little bit from where he kept it. He continued to talk about what he had learned this summer and I could tell he was very excited to try things out in his class.

We had Chinese food for lunch. Many of the teachers had much more sophisticated taste buds than myself so I considered myself lucky that I could load up on some greasy salty sesame chicken goodness. Occasionally Josh and I would split and head to fast food while the others went somewhere "fancy." David Briton who teaches US history and economics was there. David is a smart ass but he tends to use his snark for good. He knows an immense amount of trivia and also knows more about brewing beer than I did as a chemist. David had been teaching almost as long as me but he still wore a shirt and tie every day even today. He had on a yellow button-down shirt with a dark blue tie that had math equations written all over it like it was a chalkboard. Christina Gardner and Darnell Poole were both English teachers. Darnell taught AP literature while Christina taught the younger students and put together the yearbook. Darnell spoke multiple languages and travelled internationally quite a bit. His parents had quite a bit of money and so he had travelled extensively all of his life. He also would produce some of the best AP scores I've ever seen. He worked really hard for that class and his students loved him. Christina had only been hired three years before but she quickly fit in with our group.

Emily Michaels rounded out our group of eight. She taught Spanish and somehow managed to be the least mature of all of us. She was constantly finding and sharing funny memes on social media. She also had a lot of high-tech crafting gadgets that she would use for whatever hilarity or classroom decor she could come up with. The eight of us enjoyed a longer lunch since school wasn't starting for another full week. We had quite a bit of experience among ourselves and had no big rush to set up our classrooms. The others were eating grown up foods like soup and lo mein while I enjoyed some fried rice with lots of syrupy chicken and a salty layer of soy sauce.

Darnell had just returned from a trip to Ghana and Nigeria where he had stayed on the coast near Lagos. "What was your favorite food there?" asked Josh as he paused from drinking his soup.

"Probably the wood fired pizza," Darnell replied. "Didn't expect that to be my favorite but they were good. They tasted different than the ones here. The beaches were beautiful. I'd consider going back at some point but we're hoping to do our next trip to somewhere with some mountains to hike."

"I also am in favor of you taking a hike," I chimed in.

"Thanks Scott," he snarked back. "How was playing video games all summer?"

Now to be fair, I had gone a while without playing any video games. But now that my kids were old enough to play it was all coming back to me. I didn't care for many of the new games and I usually ended up finding ways to play games from when I was a kid. But I did have a fondness for the new mining block games and my wife frequently informed me that I would lose track of time playing over the summer.

"Video games are still a way for me to get paid to hang out with my kids, so literally fantastic thank you much," I finally said back after getting lost in thought.

"How much are you making off of your YouTube channel?" asked Diane.

"Not a lot, but not nothing," I responded. "In a good month between two hundred and three hundred dollars."

"Add that to your teaching salary and you're looking at an early retirement," David added.

"Correction, I get two teaching salaries," I announced loudly. "And this year mine has officially been surpassed by my wife's salary."

"Must be nice for her to work for a district that can pay their employees," muttered Emily.

"Oh, it sure is nice isn't it," I continued with a hint of being obnoxious.

"I guess you'll be paying for lunch then," said David.

"Seems communist to me," I replied and then withdrew from the conversation before I had to pay for a group of 8 hungry teachers. Emily started talking with Christine about a new logo she had designed while Mary listened. Diane and I talked briefly about cross-country practice. Diane is the head coach and I recently joined the team as her assistant. Josh and David asked Darnell advice for what they would need to do in advance in order to take a summer trip overseas. We complained about various things, and talked more about our summer vacations before slowly paying our bills and driving back to school. We had missed each other and even though we spent time complaining, we really appreciated each other's company and were glad to be back together. There were a lot of smiles as we walked into the parking lot.

Josh drove me back to school and we talked about trying to put together a staff student basketball game this year through NHS for a fundraiser. "I mean, I never made any team that I tried out for ever, but I'm still pretty confident I can beat any high school kid team," I bragged.

"Obviously," Josh replied. "If you weren't playing, I would still have the ref fix the game, but I'm trying to figure out how to get an audience there."

"We could give one extra credit point for attending and that should draw a few million students," I proposed.

"You know how much I loathe extra credit," Josh said with a slightly deeper tone.

"Too bad because while you're driving, I just tweeted out 5 extra credit points to you," I joked.

"You have a twitter???" Josh sarcastically asked. "Wow, do you have over 852 followers too?"

"8,857 at the moment," I proudly proclaimed. "And growing by the day. Soon I'll be rich."

We pulled into the parking lot and I headed straight back to my classroom to set up for the first day of class so that I'd be ready for practice after our staff meeting. My room was basically two rooms in one. We had lab benches on the outside and tables in the middle of the room that centered around the front teacher table and whiteboard. The whiteboard was interactive so it could be written on with an electronic marker. A big periodic table was covering up some of the window on the right side of the room. I set up some chemicals to start the year off and got my papers organized. I printed out a seating chart for each class so I could start matching names with faces. I took a deep breath, smiled for a second and locked the room to head to our large meeting room.

About thirty minutes after we got back, we headed to our meeting. My assistant principal Eric Fields was there setting up. While I was signing in, he approached me. "Hey Scott, how was your summer?"

"It was good, how was yours?" I asked politely, but I was already suspicious.

"Great, hey I need to meet with you about one of your students you'll have this year, can we talk after the meeting?"

"Sure, I'll hang out, but I have to make it to practice after a bit," I responded.

"Sounds good, it shouldn't take too long," Eric said as he started walking towards another teacher. Eric was overworked and was always busy. Our meeting room was filled with circular tables. I took a seat that was facing the front of the room so I could see without having to turn. As the tables filled a few teachers sat facing away from the front, boldly intending to not pay attention.

The meeting started eight minutes late. I never understood why it was so challenging to start a meeting on time. Our principal Donna Stephens started to speak. Nobody was listening. She stopped and said something to Eric. Then she loudly started a second time. Most people listened but the few that weren't continued to chat loudly. After a couple more cycles of Donna pausing and loudly proclaiming "let's get started" the meeting finally started. We were going through our goal setting procedures. Every teacher had to set a goal for the year and your goal would be how you were evaluated. This was predictably a mess. A few teachers set reasonable goals but most put together a goal that allowed them to do as little work as possible. My goal this year was to use more cognitive science with the students and to be explicit about what I was doing. Mary leaned over as Donna read a PowerPoint slide to us. "I heard a math teacher that retired put that their goal was to have students sit in their seats last year," Mary whispered to me. "They phrased it using education jargon so it didn't get caught."

Donna switched from reading to proclaiming. "Ok, let's get into groups of three and you can discuss what your goal is going to be this year. Remember a good goal can be measured, evaluated and should positively impact students!"

The room burst into noise as teachers got up to move around. It sounded like no one was talking about goals. I took this as an opportunity to talk to Eric instead of staying late. "Hey Eric," I said as I tapped him on the shoulder. "Let's talk now since it looks like we might end up here a little late."

"Oh, yeah," he started. "I had a meeting with one of the parents of a student you'll have this year." Eric looked uncomfortable. "Their daughter is going to be in your chemistry class and they had a long list of questions about your class. I just wanted to give you a heads up, the student's name is Amy Well and her mom is Karen. I got the sense that you'll hear from Karen a few times this year."

I got the sense that Eric was holding back something in order to keep the conversation professional. "Thanks for the warning," I said and I headed back to my seat. Eric went to talk to a math teacher that taught the same grade as me. I wondered if it was about the same parent. Our meeting resumed for another forty minutes of educational jargon that would be countered with a variety of teacher engagement. Finally, Donna relented and released us after a rousing speech about making a difference for every student. "All two hundred of them!" Mary whispered with a sarcastic tone.

***

After getting dressed to run, I walked out of the building. Most of the team was stretching on the sidewalk or just into the parking lot. Diane hadn't arrived yet. We met in the parking lot behind the school where students parked. We had a good size team given that school hadn't started yet. Typically, we would add a few the first two weeks of school. Our athletic wing was at the back of the school so our

13

runners would change and then wait outside until the coaches arrived. I had my new bright pink running shoes on that were hard to miss.

"Hey Coach M," Brandon said. "2 miles today and then cool down?" he asked.

"You wish," I replied. "*And I wish too,*" I thought. I was tired from last week where we'd put in almost fifty miles and my body was craving some recovery. "I actually don't know what we're doing today but we'll find out soon enough," I continued aloud. "Hopefully something we can work hard at doing."

Coach Bird was jogging over to us. "Hey everyone," she shouted. "We've been running a lot, let's do a nice easy two mile run at high tempo and do a cool down and call it a day."

"I'm going before I find out that was a joke," I yelled as I started running. A few of the faster runners quickly caught up to me in spite of a brief head start. "Let's just run to the corner of Beck and Warren and back," I let them know so I wouldn't have to pretend that I could keep up with them. As I continued to get passed by more and more runners my self-esteem took a slight dive. But it felt great to be out running. Even when my mind was busy while running, it still felt clear and easy. I ended up just behind our last group of runners by the time we got back. The first group had been stretching and chatting for a bit. The group was in a good mood after a recovery run. A few runners lingered behind and Diane stayed with them while I headed home.

Once school was up and running, I didn't have much time for playing video games but over the summer I would make videos for my YouTube channel. I tried to make a few extra videos that I could post during the school year and today was a good day to put together some work. I used to make chemistry videos but I found that posting a video of me playing video games got way more views with much less effort. I turned on the tv when I heard someone climbing down the stairs. My son came into the basement and asked if I was playing. "Sure bud," I said. "Wanna play too?" Perhaps another time will work for making a new video but I also lacked time to play with my kids during the school year at times. After about an hour I went upstairs to make dinner while he continued to play.

Tuesday we all brought in different things to have a baked potato bar. I brought bacon and had a bacon, chili and cheese baked potato with jalapenos. We had everything set up in the lounge. We had an old fridge, a couple of microwaves and a lot of tables that were a variety of heights, but we made it work.

"This was a great idea," Darnell said as he finished making a potato with sour cream, bacon and chives. He was careful not to let his tie dip into the chili.

"Thanks," I said, stealing some credit. Diane rolled her eyes at me.

"Hey did you see what we're doing tomorrow?" Josh asked.

"No, something life changing and awesome?" I asked. Sometimes I wondered if I should talk a little bit less at lunch.

"Yeah, but not quite those things at all," Josh answered. "We're going to have a meeting for 2 hours to talk about our evaluation goals and how to set them."

"I wonder how much money we spend on that total," Darnell added. He continued, "Hey so what do you guys think of this? I got an email from a parent already about how their child is not a good test taker and so they wanted to let me know that their 504 plan requires me to give them a review guide with answers a week before all of their tests. And they also can retake their tests as frequently as they would like. I went down to talk to Donna and she said she would look into it but confirmed that was what the 504 plan had written."

"Unreal," Diane said. "Do you even give tests in English where that would apply?"

"How could that have ever been written?" Josh responded in legitimate anger. "How is that even possible? I'm so sick of unreasonable demands being put into a 504, no IEP would ever be written so poorly."

"Well, you could try getting fired," I added. Josh smiled briefly before shaking his head.

"Thanks Scott, I'll think about it," Darnell stated calmly.

"I mean, it's really not so bad," I pressed. "I've been fired several times and they are usually quite gentle." A few people laughed and our lunch resumed into jovial anticipation of the school year. Our complaining was rarely us being upset and more so sharing the burden of stupid we confronted as a group so we could maintain a positive attitude while in our classes. As the conversation shifted, I briefly wondered if the parent Eric had warned me about would be in contact soon.

Our second meeting started with an icebreaker that we all could have done without. We had to stand back to back with someone, then on the count of three spin around while loudly singing a song of a specific genre. The first was a love ballad. Perhaps this sounds fun, but it was really just awkward and made everyone uncomfortable. Mary had on yet another inappropriate science shirt about doing it periodically on a table. She was getting those out of the way before the students were back but her shirt combined with her singing made me blush. After three songs we were finally allowed to sit down, and yet somehow things did not improve from there.

We got a long list of goals, methods to set goals, methods to evaluate goals and examples of bad goals. Most were clearly targeted towards elementary education. One was about how to utilize recess to your advantage as a teacher. For about thirty minutes we sat and listened. You could feel the start of the school year energy leaving the room. That combination of excitement, anxiety and stress was being displaced with annoyance and sadness.

After the lecture about goals we then got into the timelines for the year. Not only were we going to be spending hours about these goals we were going to be spending hours every month. Diane leaned over and said, "When are you supposed to grade?" I put my head down to take a break. She was right and as the sizes of our classes grew it became harder and harder to not feel discouraged.

When the meeting finally ended, we all slowly stood up and meandered towards the exit. "Well that was depressing," Emily said. Christine nodded with a pensive frown on her face. They headed back to Emily's classroom to chat but I had to go run practice.

When I got home after practice, I headed straight down to the basement to get a little bit of "work" done. I made a video showing how to defeat one of the characters as well as some ways that it can go wrong. My videos highlighted cognitive science details into how to practice at video games to maximize success. Most gamers just try doing the same thing over and over but fail to improve their brain function. I tried to think of ways to increase automated thinking via targeted practice. So far, the videos brought in way more money than I had thought they would and it was fun. I was making an extra four hundred a month on a good month so my wife was coming around to the idea. I did some editing and set the video to post around 7pm before cooking dinner.

I was tired from work so I grilled hamburgers and hot dogs. I had also just learned this new way to cook corn on the cob in the microwave in the husk and it worked really well. The cob of corn pushes out of the husk with no silk at all and it was extremely easy and convenient. After dinner I went on to my twitter account to post my new video so users that followed my teaching account would go to it. My twitter was quite polarized, switching between YouTube videos for gamers and chemistry lessons, but it was popular nonetheless. I was fast approaching 10,000 followers although many were very odd accounts. A lot of rap beat developers and also one account that just made up facts about carrots.

I posted my video on twitter and then went to clean up dinner. The whole time I washed the dishes I always thought about what would happen if I would just get a million retweets for some reason and make a million dollars on ad revenue. I knew my videos would never do that, but it was nice to dream about. After the dishes were running, I checked in and had three retweets and someone replied to my tweet saying that my head was too big for my body. Maybe next time.

Chapter 2 No Teacher Left Behind

Thursday was our final preparation day before students because Friday was a day off for everybody. I had my room ready to go, but I wanted to work on organizing my chemical supply room before I would be overwhelmed with new work to do. I technically shared the room with Diane, but I was responsible for the overwhelming majority of the mess inside. Her mess was neatly organized around her classroom. I rolled a big cart in and started putting things onto the cart, into cabinets or into the trash. After an hour and a half, I finally took a pause to get some caffeine rolling. I filled a small cup with ice and delicious cola and took it back to my classroom to read any emails while I relaxed for a minute. I had an email requesting a letter of recommendation for one of my students from last year. The problem was that she had not asked me to write it. The email was from the University. I could write the letter this weekend, but I would rather wait to be asked by the student first. I had even talked to my students at the end of the term last year about how to ask for a letter and what information I wanted and when I wanted the request by. If I didn't write it that weekend, I'd have to write it when busier, but I also wanted to make a few extra videos that I could post during the school year when I was busy. I went back to cleaning the storeroom to be productive rather than stew over it.

At lunch we just had a normal lunch, and I planned on venting, but when I got down to the lounge there were brownies and I was temporarily distracted. Then Josh walked in with a clipboard, pen and spreadsheet.

"I have an idea," he started to tell all of us. "We're going to call this, No Teacher Left Behind Club. Here's what I'm thinking. We'll start a fund where we all put in money and I'll buy a set of lottery tickets every time the Mega Millions or Powerball drawing gets beyond four hundred million dollars. There are eight of us so that would net us a cool fifty million each. But we all have to do it because it we win and someone doesn't participate, we would all quit and that teacher would be stuck here without the rest of us. I just couldn't bear to see someone suffer like that. What does everyone think?"

David responded first, "Well I assume you know about the odds of us winning."

"Right," Josh said excitedly. "They would be significantly higher with the large number of tickets we would buy as a group. Plus, only playing with large jackpots means that we are statistically likely to make more than we would spend."

"Well that's misleading, but whatever, I'm fine with it as long as it's fun," David replied.

"Think of all the fancy new ties you could buy," Emily directed him.

David adjusted his bright pink tie as if he was insulted about his current tie. "Are you insinuating that this tie isn't fancy?"

"Well this is awkward," Darnell slowly spilled out the words.

"Well if it's fun we're seeking then I think we should put some rules in to make it fun," I added. "We're probably not going to win so we should at least have bingo cards or something to make it better than just buying a bunch of losing tickets. Maybe if we win two dollars back the person who teaches chemistry the most that week wins that money."

"Or, better yet," Diane announce, "how about if win the jackpot that we split the shares nine ways and one person wins double."

"How do you win the double share?" Mary asked.

"By doing the most push-ups?" I suggested.

"Teaching contest decided by a group of disgruntled ninth graders?" Darnell posited.

"No," Diane said. The first teacher to get fired for doing something hilarious." David grinned and Mary tilted her head back laughing loudly while thinking about what she would might try and pull to get terminated.

"Oh the possibilities," I said. "That's awesome, I'll even buy the first round of tickets with my YouTube revenue for the last three days."

"Is that still making money?" Darnell asked me.

"Yep, it's pretty sweet because I could probably stop working it entirely and still pull in a couple hundred a month. But surprisingly the videos about games are still more popular than my lecture on electron configurations," I responded.

"Shocking," Donna Stephens said as she entered from the hallway. Donna was our principal, and we all were very fond of her even though as a group we probably caused her quite a bit of headaches. She always tried hard to do what was best for the students, but her job was often not conducive to being successful. Like Eric she was overworked and spread thin. But she still managed to do amazing work and it was a rare treat when she would have time to sit and chat.

"Hey Donna, thanks for finally buying us lunch," Josh goaded her.

"It's no trouble at all with my budgets," Donna snarked back. "Would you like a stringed cheese or water from the drinking fountain?" Donna had very short hair and she almost never changed her facial expression. This greatly enhanced her humor.

"I'm not fired again, am I?" I asked. Donna laughed.

"No, actually the opposite," she replied.

"You're going to punch me in the face and then make me teach ninth graders?" I asked.

"No," Donna replied, then paused in thought for an uncomfortably long time. "No that is not what I want to do currently." Then she took out a notepad and wrote down something while giggling to herself. After a moment she looked up. "No, so what I need is a new math teacher, but I have no qualified applicants. Does anyone have any connections that they could use?"

"Can they have steps on the salary schedule? Because if they can, I'll do it," I volunteered.

"You'll do no such thing," Christine replied. "You're making millions on YouTube; let us scrubs get steps for once."

"Sorry, no steps this year or next," Donna lamented. "You know the budget we're working with. Well, if you hear of anyone let us know. I can't even find a student from a university to contact at this point, so it's pretty desperate." Donna smiled and left to go back to her office while we finished lunch.

David started lecturing us, "It's awful that we've lost so much funding that the college education programs are shutting down. What are we going to do with nobody going into teaching? And I wouldn't wish it upon anyone to be honest."

"Right," I agreed. "On the flip side though I think I might be able to stop writing letters of recommendation and not get fired since they're so desperate for candidates. Can you imagine them having to hire a new chemistry teacher at this point?"

"They wouldn't need a new chemistry teacher though," Josh articulated slowly. "Just someone slightly smarter than you would suffice."

"You're lucky I'm already irritated at a student and I love your No Teacher Left Behind idea or I'd have to tell everyone that story about the last time we went drinking at the bar," I sarcastically responded and then walked out of the room feigning irritation.

"Sounds good, I'll work out the contract details, bring in sixteen dollars of YouTube winnings," Josh shouted as the door closed. I went back to my room and wrote the letter of recommendation. It felt like I had written it while angry, and I wasn't sure whether to try and improve it or not when someone knocked on my classroom door and opened it.

A woman walked in that I did not recognize. "Mr. Miles" she asked inquisitively.

"That's me, can I help you?" I responded with curiosity.

"Hi, my name is Karen, my daughter Amy Well is going to be in your first hour chemistry class this year. I was hoping we could talk for a minute," Mrs. Well said as she sat down clearly intending to have a meeting regardless of what I was doing.

This must be the parent that Eric was trying to warn me about. I looked at the clock and saw that I had about ninety minutes until I had to leave for practice. "Sure," I said. I was trying to gather my thoughts about how to best play this meeting. Should I act tough and set a tone that I wasn't to be messed with or should I keep things quick and try and keep her happy with minimal interaction?

"I was just hoping to get Amy on the right track for your class. I know it's a challenging one and I want her to do well. And I really love chemistry, it was my favorite class in school and I want her to enjoy it rather than be frustrated as she learns it," Karen explained.

That sounded pretty reasonable to me. I was waiting for a catch but that was all that she had to say. "Sure, I'm not quite prepared at the moment but I'll show you where our resources are and I have a book that I'm reading right now that I'm planning to

use as a class philosophy sort of for the year." I
showed our class website, emailed her a link along
with the title of the book I borrowed from Josh about
cognitive science. Karen thanked me and then
apologized for interrupting my work and left. I was
suspicious because of Eric's warning but I relaxed
after she left.

I moved to the supply room and started
organizing everything into piles to clean. Diane burst
in right as I had made things from bad to worse.

"What did you do in here?" she shouted.

"Oh, sorry, I'm in the middle of cleaning," I
apologized. "I just had to write this letter real quick so
I don't work over the weekend and a parent just came
in for a conference."

"Sorry?" she laughed. "This storeroom has
room to move around for once. I love it." I wiped an
imaginary bead of sweat from my brow. "Do you want
some help finishing it?" she offered.

"Sounds great," I answered. "Let's clean it now
before the school year and cross-country season
make it a next year project."

"How did you have a conference already?" She
asked.

I explained to her about my discussion with
Eric and described the meeting that had just
happened. We cleaned and talked about who we
hoped our principal, Donna, would hire for math while
we inefficiently removed the mess. I went home a bit
later and did not even think about school until it was
the night before Monday. The night before the first

day of school still got to me, although not nearly as badly as it used to when I was new. I used to struggle to fall asleep and just lay awake thinking about how little sleep that I was getting the night before the first day of school. In spite of that, I would never be tired the first day, but I would feel it on Thursday of that week. I looked at my clock several times without falling asleep. I knew better than to try to go to bed too early, but I figured by 11 I would already be less than seven hours of sleep. By 1am I was down to about four and a half hours, and at some point, I finally slept for what seemed like two hours. I still managed to wake up just before my alarm went off and got ready.

Every year I planned to go over the syllabus and start learning my students' names, but every year I backed out at the last minute and would do a small science experiment. This year I just quit on the syllabus completely. Students had to be sick of hearing teachers speak about how strict they were all day. So I took a long glass tube and put a small amount of flammable isopropanol in it. Then I turned all of the lights down and lit the tube from the bottom end using a candle. A flame formed inside of the tube but then moved up and down erratically with an occasional spooky noise emanating from the tube. The class was silent until the first noise happened and some whispers of excitement formed. That was followed by shushing that covered up the rest of the noises. The flame had moved to the top of the tube and looked like an unusual torch before the flame entered back into the tube and shifted around before slowly fading out.

"Can you do it again?" a student in the back asked after the flame had disappeared.

"Nope," I responded. "Why can't I do this again?" The room was quiet for a while. I let them stay quiet until it started to get uncomfortable. "Fair enough, turn to the person sitting next to you, learn their name and try and come up with an idea of why it won't work to try and light this on fire again." The room slowly increased in volume as students talked out some ideas. I told the students to take their ideas they had and put them onto a whiteboard by drawing the firetube but showing what is happening inside at the particle level. They worked in groups of four for the rest of the time drawing their ideas.

At lunch I walked in feeling like I had done a decent job teaching. It was just the first day, but I liked starting with something enjoyable. Josh met me at the door to the lounge.

"I tried something new today for the first day, it was pretty good," he said as we walked in. "I had the students make a map of the room to scale but with two different scales. So one group made a map and the other had to end up with a map twice as large."

"I like it," I said. "Did they include your book collection?"

"Yep, all three of them were included," he responded.

"Oh, so I brought in our lottery starter kit," I said and reached into my pocket to get my wallet. I pulled out sixteen dollars and a quarter. "I included a tip as well so you can buy yourself something nice," I said and then winked suggestively.

"Are we rich yet," asked Diane. "I'm getting impatient about not waking up before 6am."

"Actually, I made a spreadsheet, typed up a contract and made a dropbox shared with all of us to post pictures of the tickets purchased prior to the drawings. So at this point I was just waiting on Scott to finally get us rolling and for the winnings to get high enough that it's worth our while. No point in only winning a few million you know," Josh explained.

"A few million is completely beneath my social standing," I agreed.

"What's our staff meeting about today," Darnell asked shifting the topic.

"I'm hoping it's finally a trophy presentation for best chemistry teacher," I said while no one listened. Sometimes I wondered if I talked too much at lunch.

"It's to show us how to use the new data analysis software," Christine replied.

"I love how we can afford new data software, but I get thirty dollars for supplies for 177 students," said Emily. "That's about fifteen cents per student. Here's your piece of paper and two paper clips."

"No es bueno," I said with an impressive Spanish accent.

"Sí!" Emily replied before realizing she was about to slip into her Spanish teaching mode where she spoke in an overly enthusiastic tone for emphasis. "I mean, yes."

"Technically the money for the new software comes from the county, not our school funds," David corrected us. He had on a white button-down shirt with his 1st day of school tie. "The new software is pretty useful. It would be more useful if we had better laptops and better training, but it's a start."

"Can you just let us vent without having to be correct about everything?" Christine responded.

"When did you train on it?" Emily asked.

"We got a release over the summer to train, but it was a mess," David responded. "They had us make a test and then take the test to get data instead of analyzing actual student results. The person running the training had only seen the program the day before and so everything was basic and was delivered very slowly."

"That's weird, I did the exact same lesson with my students today," I commented. This time smiles happened and a couple of people laughed. Maybe I didn't talk too much!

"Hey you said something funny," Josh remarked. "Put it on your trophy that you're getting later!"

I stood up and gave Josh a high five before giving a large curtsy to the group and headed back to my classroom. I wanted to stretch for a bit before going to the meeting so I would be less tight for running after. Being on my feet for a few hours always messed me up when we transitioned from summer practices to practice after school. I did some foam rolling and stretches with every window covered so no one could see me laying down on the floor in mesh shorts.

***

I walked in about three minutes before the meeting started so the room was nearly empty besides our principal Donna Stephens and our assistant principal Eric Fields. Eric walked over to say hello, and he and I chatted about the cross-country team for a bit. Donna was trying to get our sound system functional, which was the norm for our staff meetings. Soon a very long line formed at the entrance to the room where the sign-in sheet was. The volume in the room quickly grew as teachers coming from lunch chatted loudly. No one sat down and it was about three minutes after when we were supposed to start the meeting that a loud microphone feedback shriek interrupted everything. It was probably the most effective way to get everyone to shut up to be honest.

We sat down and the PowerPoint began. Part of me hated meetings like these and part of me liked finding new things to add to my teaching. The part that won out frequently depended on who I was sitting with. Today I sat by Eric instead of the usual crew, and I paid close attention. Unfortunately, the PowerPoint was not very well put together. We had to stop and have David explain things multiple times, and it didn't really connect with the way I did grading anyways. I was glad when it was time for practice and

I snuck out the side door and jogged to the front of the building to meet the team.

Diane was talking to the team as I approached. I joined the crowd listening to her as she talked about expectations for meets, schedules and diet. I added in my tip for eating soft pretzels as a great pre-race meal much to her dismay. This was not the first time I presented those soft delicious bundles of carbs, and I stuck with my anecdotal evidence in spite of her push for pasta. We split up the team into two squads and Diane took the slower runners out on a 4 mile loop while I took the faster runners on an eight mile run. It was four miles out and four miles back, so I turned around when the last runner had passed me on their way back. I ended up going just over seven miles and I felt decent but definitely tired. Around mile five I remembered that I had to make a plan for teaching the next day. I had an experiment to do, but it wasn't set up. I could delay the lab and do a worksheet, but I hadn't made copies of it. Either way it was going to be an early start to the day.

When I got home, I checked my email and had one from Karen Well.

Hello Mr. Miles,
I have five syllabi for Amy but I did not receive one for chemistry. Is she going to get it tomorrow or is it posted somewhere?
Thanks!
Karen

I had a few things to work on for tomorrow so I quickly sent a response that we weren't using one this year and so if she had any questions to just send me a response with them.

I woke up early to go in and set up the experiment. It was too early to skip over an experiment for a worksheet, and I'd survive losing twenty minutes of sleep. Maybe it would even help me get used to waking up early again. The experiment was to measure the mass and volume of a set of blocks. Each group got their own material with a set of blocks of various sizes. What I had them do was measure the masses and volumes, then plot the data points and find a line of best fit. Then we analyzed what the y-intercepts were and spent a lot of time working out what the slopes were, why they were different for different substances and how to use them. It was a simple experiment, but it helped students establish some procedures for analyzing data that we would use throughout the year. At the end of the discussion, I pulled out two blocks both made of wood. I showed them that the one block floated in water, but the second had several holes drilled out of it. I asked what would happen with the second and let them argue about it. Somehow, we managed to not get to testing it in every hour, so it turned into a teaser for tomorrow's class.

At lunch we had all brought in food for tacos. I had carne asada made by a local restaurant. Diane had made chicken and everyone else brought in the fixings and tortillas. I made one taco of each.

Sometimes our food gatherings were foods that I wasn't that into, but taco day was legit. I had bacon, salsa, lettuce, cheese, taco sauce with a little bit of green peppers and jalapenos. I avoided the chips and went back for a second round of tacos. Nobody brought dessert because we all knew we just wanted the tacos.

"This is awesome," exclaimed Mary. She was wearing a t-shirt with a frothy mixture in a beaker that said "You're overreacting" and in solidarity I had on my shirt that said "Never trust an atom, they make up everything."

"I still say one of these should be a pizza or fast food potluck," I shared.

"Why are you the way that you are?" Darnell said slowly.

"Lots of steroids," I suggested while shrugging. "I call them teacher performance enhancing supplements."

"That's not a bad idea," Josh joined in.

"Thanks!" I said.

"Just kidding, it's a terrible idea and you should feel bad," Josh's voice turned. I hung my head in shame. The mood was good in the room. Donna walked in. "I didn't say it and you can't prove that I did," Josh announced to her.

"Relax Josh, oooh tacos?" Donna responded while raising her eyebrows seeking an invite for a plate.

"Of course we're sharing with our favorite principal," I said. Sometimes I tried to be a bit nicer to

Donna because I had to be a headache for her at times. She didn't seem upset the time I filled the hall with smoke from a fiery experiment gone wrong, but there has to be a limit to her patience eventually.

"Carne asada? That was my favorite when I lived in California as a kid," Donna exclaimed. "OK, before I get completely distracted, I need help. I still can't fill our open teaching spot, and I will continue to come steal free food until I can. Does anyone know a math teacher in another district that might consider moving closer to get a better drive or a retired teacher or someone with a pulse that will work for entry level pay?"

"You could double up Josh's classes and pay him an extra sub pay per hour," Emily pleasantly announced.

"You could double up your...," Josh's voice trailed off as he remembered Donna was in the room. Josh also caused a few headaches for her over the years. We always tried to appreciate her patience by helping her out when we could. It seemed though that the growing teacher shortage was beyond our capabilities to help.

"Well if anyone can find someone, it would really help out my ability to fire Josh," Donna lamented and then left with a full plate of tacos. I checked the clock and realized that I had to run back to class to finish some paperwork. I always hated leaving lunch early, but during season, time was in short supply and high demand.

I especially wasn't thrilled with doing paperwork for the annual pretend you have a new goal that fits every single criteria of the district without them explicitly telling you what your goal is. It's frustrating because I had goals and wanted to get better at teaching. And I did those things, I worked hard at getting better. But the disingenuous nature of these state implemented reforms were a downer. This was my second revision because my goal did not cover a specific unit that had to be included. So now I was submitting a really phony goal that was not as good but met the criteria better. I would have finished too, but a student came in early to ask about what she should do when she was on vacation next week and after that, class was nearly ready to start.

I finished after school before practice started and felt mildly accomplished, but also felt stretched thin. I talked to Diane before we got running, and we agreed that we could both use a practice off occasionally to get caught up with school work. We preached that to the runners, but that advice seemed sage for us as well. I let Diane run the practice and I headed home. It was still the first week, but I took both kids out to play miniature golf while it was nice out and then we went to a park to play for a while.

Sometimes, as summer winds down, you can look forward to having some separation from the kids, but it was also a short time before the Michigan winter kicked in and the kids would get bored being inside all day. Plus, they had started school as well. It was a nice break even for the first week. We grabbed fast food on the way home and of course everyone chose tacos. It was good, but not taco potluck for lunch good.

Before going to bed I checked my email. Karen had already responded.

Hi Mr. Miles,
I don't know if I can easily narrow down my questions. Would you be able to type up a syllabus for us to use or perhaps send us one from last year?

Thanks,
Karen

I laughed at the idea of making a syllabus for a single student. I decided I had better wait on replying until tomorrow and see if I could think of a more reasonable solution.

Chapter 3 Breakfast for lunch

By week two we had a lottery fund going, and if no one won the Powerball drawing on Saturday the jackpot would officially be over four hundred million. We decided to celebrate our winnings in advance with a breakfast for lunch meal. I had a lot of ideas and decided they were all within the budget. I brought in an assortment of my favorite pastries that could be cooked in a toaster along with my very fancy toaster. Emily brought in sausage and bacon, which went great with the strawberry strudels in my humble opinion. It made a great combination of salty and sweet. Mary made scrambled eggs with cheese and Josh went all out this time bringing in a griddle that he used to make crepes. I caved and tried one with strawberries. It was ok, but I felt my dishes were yet again underappreciated.

"What this breakfast really needs is a nap afterwards," David shared.

"How do you say breakfast in Spanish?" Christine asked Emily.

"Desayuno," Emily replied.

"I have this student who I found out speaks fluent Spanish in my third hour but is not able to take Spanish because they don't have any spare electives this year because of band. I felt bad so I told her I would learn some Spanish," Christine explained.

"Definitely one word should cover a conversation, for sure," I teased. "Hola Señora Christine, cómo estás hoy? Desayuno. Como fue tu fin de semana? Desayuno."

"Hey, Emily, how do I say shut the hell up Scott in Spanish?" Christine asked loudly.

Emily without changing expression said, "Callate tu boca señor feo."

"Your mom is feo," I whispered sheepishly.

"So, I got another email," David interrupted us. "This one the student wants to know if I can get together all of their work for November because they're going on an international cruise and they don't want to fall behind."

"I want to go on an international cruise. Where are they going?" asked Mary. Mary had on a t-shirt with a picture of a bone that said "I find this humerus."

"They said you can't go," Josh announced.

"Finland, Denmark and Norway for the cruise and then they fly to Italy for a week," David responded. "So not only do I not get to go on a trip, I get to do extra work for them to go."

"Bummer, but remember that if nobody wins this weekend, out first lottery drawing will be next week and we could all be going on a trip to Italy," Josh said.

"I'm pretty sure we'll win the first time we play too," I concluded. "Seems only fair since yesterday I picked up a piece of garbage off the floor that wasn't even mine."

"That's some good karma there Scott, well done," Darnell said with deep admiration.

"Hah, I have even better karma," Diane added. "I have had three long emails from a parent about how hard their child is trying in physics and how they've always been an A student and I managed to keep it together when their precious genius fell asleep again today in class. Must have been the stress of his straight A, 2.64 GPA he's been working so hard at. They keep trying to ask questions about class so they can do his homework for him. I'm very convinced his lab report was not written by him."

"Just start sending the grades and feedback directly to the parent," I suggested.

"You won't do it," Josh added.

Diane sighed. "If we win the lottery, I'll email a picture of the kid sleeping," she promised as a compromise.

"Deal!" both Josh and I exclaimed and then he punched me in the arm. We cleaned up the big mess we had made with our breakfast at lunch during the last ten minutes of lunch.

"It's kind of ironic that we're having a breakfast luncheon but we eat lunch when lots of people are just eating breakfast," Darnell observed.

"Ahhh the perks of waking up before 5:30 am," I said.

"5:30? You get to sleep until 5:30?" Josh asked incredulously.

"No, before 5:30, 5:28 this morning," I corrected him.

"In the winter I have to get up by 4:45 to make it when it's snowing," Mary lamented.

"You should consider living within two miles of the school," I recommended.

"Not worth it, I never have to see a parent or student outside of school hours," Josh responded.

"It's not so bad, it's like being a mini-celebrity," I added. "I mean unless it interferes with your cocaine addiction."

"Better than teacher performance enhancing drugs," David remarked.

"They're called teacher performance enhancing essential oils," I responded quickly and quietly. "No need to bring out the "d" word." I winked and then headed back to class and got there just before class started. It was really nice to have quality lunch time but bringing in food like that did put an even bigger time crunch on us than usual.

That weekend we had an invitational for our freshman runners only. Cross-country invitationals were pretty fun; the track ones in the spring were absurdly long and you were going to lose the entire day. Cross-country had two races and those were both over in under an hour total. Between bus rides, warm ups, cool downs and trophies the whole thing was about three hours. Since they started early in the morning, I was home just after noon and got to work grading. I tried to grade something the first three weeks because it helped me learn students' names. Learning names had become quite the difficulty since I began teaching. We were getting over one hundred seventy students a year. I also had about sixty athletes to learn between track and cross-country. The first three weeks my brain would change rapidly, and I could feel the names from last year slipping out.

Occasionally I would become unable to recall an athlete's name that I had in class the year before. I started keeping old seating charts so I could look the name up later and make sure I could still recall it.

Sunday morning, I checked and sure enough the lottery was up to five hundred forty-five million. We would be playing for the first time in week three. I had never really done the lottery growing up, so it was new and exciting to me. I liked playing even though I wasn't going to win because I enjoyed envisioning winning the day before. It was like paying two dollars to go to a movie but the movie was me daydreaming about a similar but monetarily enhanced life. I was pretty sure that if I won, I would have to keep teaching but with some major changes. I don't think I could just not work all of my life even if I had the money. I was too young to retire. What I would do for sure though is get an administrative assistant to do all of the lousy parts of teaching. They would respond to emails, do most of the grading, do lab set up and lab clean up. I would just get to do the fun parts: creative lessons, teaching, interacting with students. I would be a generous rich person too and share my assistant with other teachers on occasion.

Monday was a review day since Tuesday was the test. My dreams only lingered slightly as I anticipated the joy of grading 170 exams this week. Grading that number of anything was tough, but these weren't multiple-choice exams and they took a quality chunk of time to read through and evaluate. It was going to be rough. Tuesday was a long day of staring at kids as they frantically filled out their tests. Between 2nd and 3rd hour two of the students took so long that I didn't have time to run to the bathroom. By the time 3rd hour was done I was more than ready for a break. Every hour the stack that needed to be graded became a large chunk larger.

At lunch I started grading but I still had to eat. By the time I had made an answer key and eaten I only got through a few tests. During my prep I got through a few more but they were slow and after school I had to rush to make the bus to a cross-country meet.

By the time we got to Thursday I was struggling. For our group lunch we had picked subs. I brought in meatballs for some meatball subs. Others brought in lunch meats, cheeses, toppings and David brought in fancy bread for the subs. It was good and I had some chips and pop with a meatball sub with salami on top.

"Well did we win yet," Diane prodded at Josh.

"I posted the tickets on the dropbox, and you see I'm still wearing pants, so clearly we did not," Josh replied with a touch of saltiness in his voice.

"Well I would like to say, that even though we suffered a setback, I enjoyed the thought of no pants Josh," I added.

"Getting uncomfortable here," Mary said and threw her hands up in the air. Mary had on a shirt that said "I heart biology" but the heart was a human heart.

"Fortunately, nobody won, so Saturday night it is," David informed us. He was wearing a tie that had a map of the world on it with a white button-down shirt. I sat at lunch quietly and thought about how I was glad we were playing and how two bucks was a cheap price for some quality conversation with good friends.

"I checked the spreadsheet and everyone is paid up for a few more rounds but feel free to just bring in more money whenever," Josh added.

"I'm glad you're still taking IOUs," Diane joked.

"Just like my homework policy," Josh said back.

"What's homework?" Diane asked with a confused look on her face. I grabbed another sub to eat after my next class and headed to go try and submit my goals for a third time.

As I walked out Josh was saying, "Your homework is to figure out how 670 million dollars splits up eight ways when we win this weekend."

After I got my goals submitted, I quickly shifted thinking back to grading. I really did not like to have tests sitting ungraded, but I was only through about eighty because of the meet on Tuesday and then Wednesday my kids both had soccer practice. The priority had been driving errands and dinner. I was actually impressed that I got through 80, but I still was not even halfway there. I graded a couple in between every class and by the afternoon I made it past halfway. I had extra stress because I had received an email from Karen Well asking when I thought I would be done grading the tests. I thought about asking Diane if I could run from practice early to grade but she asked me if she could go to her kids' school for a party they were having first. I told her of course but after she left, I decided to let the kids run on their own today and I hung back and kept grading. By Friday I was onto the final class and Saturday they were done. It felt good to be done but I needed a break again. I had been grading non-stop all week and I was exhausted. Reading the thoughts of 170 new chemistry students was what I imagined a marathon felt like for my brain, and I had hit the wall.

I slept in Sunday and did a fat lot of nothing for a while. I probably should have stretched, gone running, exercised, planned some lessons or did some chores but the lazy bug was hitting hard. Soon it was the afternoon and I had wasted most of the day and still felt like I had graded for five straight days every spare minute. I checked my email as I sat around and the complaints were coming in.

Dear Mr. Miles,
We saw that Bill didn't do so well on his first exam and we were wondering what we should do to improve.

Mr. Miles,
I've been concerned about the lack of homework in your class and saw that Jan did poorly on the first test. Where should we go to find more practice?

Is there a way for Mike to get extra credit to improve his grade?

Hey Mr. Miles, my parents want me to ask you about my test on Monday and if I can retake it.

I could spend all day responding to these. I went and cleaned up the house and figured I had done enough school work for the week and should probably focus on planning the agenda for the week before emailing. It felt like many emails were just there to dump the stress parents and kids had onto me. I get it, but I don't have the mental strength to carry around the grade anxiety of 170 students. Hopefully lunch with the crew would provide some mental therapy. We probably complained about emails a minimum of once a month and the first set of test grades meant we'd all have a bunch.

We had decided that Thursday would be our lunch day every week so that we could celebrate our lottery failings with a big lunch. Monday I had nothing to bring leftover so it was a microwave pizza for me. It was not good either. I don't know why as an adult I couldn't bring myself to buy the four dollar pizza instead of the one that was less than a dollar. But spending four dollars on a pizza that was a single felt wasteful. I regretted my decision and vowed this would be the final time I did it. My pizza added to a bitter mood I was in. Teaching definitely put me through some highs and lows. It was a lot to keep track of and I was not feeling it at the moment. The grading had been long and I was never ready for the backlash of parents and students following all of that hard work. It just was exhausting and made me feel unappreciated, even if the intentions were to help students. It felt like trying to avoid doing things they should do and also trying to weasel out of their role in everything. I sat quietly for lunch and I don't think anybody noticed. They were probably glad I wasn't making obnoxious comments for once.

After school there was a knock on my door and before I could answer Karen Well walked in. "Hello Mr. Miles," she announced. I was surprised to see her as she had no appointment and I was also growing weary of the contact. I had already had about seven email exchanges with her.

"Hi Mrs. Well, I was about to go to practice in a minute," I started to explain.

"Then I'll get right to the point," she interrupted. "I'm concerned about Amy's first test grade and was hoping to get some feedback on how she should improve." My stress levels were quickly rising.

"Why don't you send her to talk to me tomorrow and I will try and give her some feedback," I responded. Josh had done well to convince me two years ago that it was always better to discuss grades with the student and not the parent.

"Sure," Karen said in a disappointed tone with a hint of annoyance. "But I also drove all the way here, could I look over her mistakes quickly?" she asked.

"I'm afraid that won't work," I responded. "The tests are common in the department and also I have to get going to practice." I stood up and grabbed my running clothes to change into. Karen looked like she was deciding whether to argue with me about my schedule that she had interrupted with no notice again. So I quickly grabbed my keys and started locking my door to help persuade her to leave. "Make sure to send Amy to talk to me," I reminded her. She nodded and left with obvious annoyance painted on her face. I walked down to the athletic wing and got changed, but I was now eight minutes early to practice and no one was there yet. My irritation was growing and I felt silly for not recognizing Karen's aggression when she showed up unannounced before school had even started. Eric had warned me.

No one won the lottery on Saturday so the jackpot had grown to 883 million dollars. I think at a certain point you could just buy enough lottery tickets to guarantee you win, but it would take too long to fill out the cards or something. I took Monday off from pretty much everything. I responded to emails grudgingly and I ran at practice, but then I bought Chinese food for dinner and did no work the entire night. I felt a bit better. Tuesday we did an experiment where we changed the pressure of a gas by heating and cooling it. We plotted the pressure vs. temperature on a whiteboard and found the line of best fit. Then we got into a big circle and talked about everything. We talked about what the slope was, why the pressure got bigger when temperature got bigger and why the intercept wasn't zero. This evolved into the need for a different temperature scale besides Celsius where the intercept would be zero. We wanted a temperature scale where zero meant no motion of the particles. It was a good lesson with a lot of thinking and again I felt better. Unfortunately, I had to meet again about my goals with Donna. I didn't mind meeting, in fact it was nice to get to spend time with Donna who was very overworked, but that meant I had no time to catch up on email and setting up tomorrow's experiment.

I sat down in the seat in the entrance to Donna's office where her secretary Maurice worked. Maurice was awesome, but he was as busy as Donna was, so we almost never saw him. "Hey Scott," Maurice greeted me. "She's ready in there."

"Thanks, I just want to sit and do nothing for like thirty seconds and then I'm heading in," I responded.

Maurice laughed jovially. "Not a problem. I might do that after you leave; it's one of those days."

I stood up and walked into Donna's office and sat down at her desk. She was leaving a message with someone on the phone, and I was too worn out to even try and listen for some gossip.

"Hey Scott," Donna quickly transitioned back to me. "How are your kids at home doing?"

"Good, good," I replied. "I mean, I'm a bit overwhelmed and wish I had more time to spend with them, but they're good." I always felt stupid when I complained about being busy to Donna since she did much more than I ever did.

"Great, so listen, I'm sorry the goal process takes so long to complete," Donna spoke quickly. "I know you've been revising quite a bit, but they make changes and I don't always have a complete say in how those changes are going to get implemented. But I think we're all set for the year now and I should be around to watch your room soon for an observation."

"Today was pretty good. In fact, I think this week in general is a good set of lessons that you'd enjoy observing," I added. "I'm working on getting the students to do a bit more challenging thinking and it's going well so far."

Donna smiled and said, "Don't ever leave Mr. Miles, I don't know how I'd replace you. Especially right now."

"Thanks Donna. Hey if you're busy I'm good and can head back to do some set up," I suggested.

"That sounds good," she replied. "I look forward to being in the classroom instead of the amazingly fun things I'm doing now."

"Hey, just so you know we've been doing group lunches on Thursday, so find an excuse to stop by sometime," I said on my way out. "That goes for you too Maurice, come hang out with us once in a while. You're busy working in here all day long and it's good to have a break once in a while."

"Thanks!" Maurice said. "I'll try and do that, sounds like fun and I could use some fun this week." I quickly walked back to my room and reset the lab for my next hour while also getting the equipment for tomorrow's experiment out. I was glad to not have to wake up early the next day.

By Wednesday I felt like I was getting my life back together a little bit, but also felt a bit worn from this week. It's hard to recover during the week, which is why it's so important to rest on Sunday a bit. At lunch we checked in on our "No Teacher Left Behind" lottery agreement. We were all set for payments and Josh had already procured us a set of tickets and shared the pictures in the dropbox. "Should we buy double the tickets since the jackpot is so high?" Darnell asked.

"No, better to stretch those funds out," Josh replied. "I assure you that there will be plenty of jackpots worth winning over the course of the school year. What's most important is that everyone flushes ice and or twenty-dollar bills down the toilet tonight before the drawing."

"That's your solution to everything," I stated.

"Speaking of solutions to everything, listen to the scam I just pulled," David explained. "So I've been casually increasing my mustache, little bit little, for the last two weeks. Then today I shaved it." David had never had a mustache, and I hadn't noticed him growing one.

"I don't get it," Mary responded. Mary had on a shirt with a cell taking a selfie that said "Cell-fie."

"The students will think I had a mustache and then I'll pretend like I never did have one," he exclaimed excitedly.

"What?" Josh responded. We all looked stumped.

"Ok, so today this kid in my 2nd hour asked what happened to my mustache," David continued explaining. "And I looked at him like he was stupid and said that I never had a mustache. He must be confusing me with someone else."

"You put way too much effort into this scheme," Darnell laughed. "Whatever that is."

"Do your parents screen your phone calls?" Diane asked David.

"Shut up," David sulked. "I thought it was funny." It was weird for me to see someone else try too hard to be funny and come up short. I got up to leave and Diane reminded me that tomorrow was ice cream sundae day.

***

When I woke up, I got ready a little faster than normal and went downstairs to check if anyone had purchased a winning ticket. I fumbled around trying to search and found that no one had won and no one in Michigan had won any major prizes. At least the jackpot would continue to grow, but it was another three days of dreaming about winning instead of planning interviews for my new butler. I had bought a bunch of candy to mix in with ice cream for sundae bar and I also wanted something to eat besides ice cream. I took some strawberries and a salami sandwich with cheese. Today in class we were starting to do calculations for pressure changes for volume, amount and temperature. It was a pretty easy lesson. I had read this summer that when students don't know how to solve a problem it's the best time for them to do some quality learning. I decided to try it out and was going to have them all try problem one in groups and then compare answers with another group.

They worked out problems in groups and a number of students were complaining. I recalled that the book had said something about how when people learn well that they feel less confident in their learning. Every single group worked out the problem correctly with good methods but satisfaction was low. I had a group show everyone what they had done and let students ask questions. Some groups used proportional reasoning and a few groups had constructed equations from the graphs we had done earlier in the week. They both worked fine and most students preferred the proportional reasoning. I told them to try the remaining problems by themselves or working in pairs.

When it was time for lunch, I got down right away since I had an easy day. I pulled the ice cream out of the freezer so it could soften a little bit before we added our candies. There were brownies from David, bananas from Darnell, strawberry slices and hot fudge from Diane, whipped cream from Emily and the rest had brought ice cream and containers. I had brought a large variety of candy toppings. I had every name brand candy bar you could think of plus toffee, chocolate chips, crushed up cookies and gummy bears. As I finished setting up Diane and Josh walked in.

"So the good news is, the jackpot is now over one billion dollars," Josh was saying.

"I make that much on YouTube in December," I scoffed.

"That account is inappropriate to talk about at school," Diane joked.

"A billion dollars though, that's enough to split up amongst eight people and have a lot for everybody," I said.

"How can you handle being so smart and being with us normal intellect people?" Diane said in awe of my logic and reasoning.

"Hey easy there Diane," I said. That was her second dig at me and we hadn't even opened the ice cream yet. She smiled and winked at me. "I think we're both going to have to do some distance at practice today," I said while making myself a bowl of ice cream with more candy than any mere mortal could tolerate.

"Are you sure you'll be able to run when you have diabetes from this one bowl of candy with ice cream?" Emily asked me.

"I'll manage," I responded proudly. "So I was thinking some more about it, if we had a billion dollars we could have one thousand piles of a million dollars and we could choose the piles of million dollars we wanted like a draft."

"That'd be a good YouTube video," Darnell suggested.

"I'll get on that as soon as we get the piles on Sunday," I assured him.

"Don't forget about the taxes that would come out; that would take away a lot of the piles first," Christine reminded me.

"Perhaps, but I think I'll still manage to have enough to get by," I concluded. The rest of lunch we spent giving Emily advice on what classes she should take for her master's degree. She was hoping to start in the winter and get a pay bump within a couple of years.

After school I headed to practice and felt better yet again. I was a bit tired, but school had been a reasonable workload today. There had been a bit more whining than I care for, but good learning had taken place and I was ready to run off some ice cream. We ran five miles at a decent clip and all of a sudden it was just Friday left before the weekend. I was also a bit excited that the lottery was over a billion. I know it was still unlikely, but for some reason the jackpot being over a billion made it even more exciting. I thought about staying up late on Saturday to watch the drawing but I needed some sleep.

When I woke up on Sunday morning there were no winners yet again. A few tickets for a million had won where they match all of the numbers except for one, but the one in Michigan that had won was in the UP. Josh had bought the tickets on Thursday and told us at lunch on Friday, so I was sure he hadn't gotten them five hours north of us. But yet again the jackpot got even bigger. So many people had bought tickets to win the billion that the new jackpot was up to 1.8 billion. I figured this Wednesday would probably be the final day we buy lottery tickets for a bit as someone would surely win. Too many people would play and too many office pools like ours would happen for no one to win. I was surprised the jackpot had made it this high. It had only been over a billion a few times.

I transitioned into Monday's lessons. We had done a good job the week before and now we were going to do some real-world applications of gas pressure. Monday was fun demonstration day. I crushed a can, inflated a balloon into a flask inside out, we did the ammonia fountain, made some smoke with hydrochloric acid and ammonia and I did a magic trick where I used pressure to make it seem like water would magically refill into a container. Then at the end of the hour we got out a vacuum pump and bell jar and made balloons to inflate with funny faces on them. It was a blast and I was officially recovered from grading the week before. The students spent the final ten minutes coming up with one detailed explanation they were comfortable giving for one of the demonstrations as well as one demonstration that they weren't sure how to explain. I received yet another email from Mrs. Karen Well that evening.

Dear Mr. Miles,
Amy thoroughly enjoyed the activities in class today. However, we were not quite sure what the purpose of the lesson was and we want to make sure Amy does

not fall further behind on her grades. Could you send us a summary of the key points and concepts that will be tested?
Thanks so much!
Karen

I wanted to write back that perhaps she should let her daughter, who is extremely capable, figure out what she's supposed to know. I searched the email inbox and this was the 12th email I had received on top of two surprise conferences. If I spent half this much time on every student, I would never teach anything. I sent back a reply telling Karen to have Amy talk with me after Wednesday's lesson if she still felt uncertain and hoped that would suffice.

Tuesday we put everything together and did some review practice looking over some basics for the calculations and some questions about pressure that dealt with conceptual scenarios like we had done the day before. Then Wednesday we did a quiz that asked students to do some calculations. I thought about having them explain a demonstration, but I was still feeling the recovery period from grading last week. So instead I wrote a new quiz that either had mathematical problems to solve or multiple-choice questions that dealt with the conceptual components. I got over half of them graded before I left for practice. Then I finished them up easily at home since they took very little effort to mark. When I finished, I transitioned back into thinking about the lottery drawing that would be happening that night.

It was stupid, but before I went to bed, I thought a bit about what would it be like if we won the lottery the next day. It would be such an inordinate amount of money for all of us. Would I stop teaching? Would we move? I loved my life and the thought of having such big changes available seemed a bit daunting. But that was foolish. I knew in the back of my head it would never happen. Maybe we would get all of the numbers except for one and split a million dollars though.

The next day I woke up and checked the reports to see if a winning ticket had been sold. There was one sold but it was in Kentucky. Oh well. It was still fun to think about an alternate life. I got dressed and pretended that I didn't know we had lost for just a couple more hours. I knew the jackpot would build back up soon and that we would be able to have fun joking about winning in the meantime.

Chapter 4 The Meeting

I got a text message on the drive in, but didn't want to check it while driving. I hoped that everything was okay since it's odd to get a message at 6:30 in the morning. I worried that my kids were sick, and I started thinking of some alternate plans just in case. When I got into my parking spot I checked and the message was from Josh. He said he needed us to all meet with him in his room before school and that it was urgent. I didn't know what to make of that, but I was relieved that I could carry on with my original lesson plans for the day. Emily was getting out of her car as I grabbed my things and we walked into school together.

"Hola, buenos días," I said.

"Not ready for that yet," she replied. "It's gonna take some café before we start with the español."

"Fair enough," I said. "For the record I am primed and ready to discuss any chemistry problems that you're curious about even without caffeine."

Emily laughed. "Yeah, I'll let you know." One of her students was walking towards the front door and said hello.

"Hola Jenna," Emily replied to her.

"What was that about?" I asked Emily. "I thought you needed coffee before speaking Spanish!"

"I know, I know, I need help," she replied. "What do you think this meeting with Josh is about?" she asked.

"You got that text message too?" I asked.

"The one just a few minutes ago," she said. "Yeah, it was you, me and a few others."

"Weird, hopefully he's okay," I said, now with a bit of concern. "Too bad the winning lottery tickets were in Kentucky or I'd be excited," I joked.

"That was my first thought as well. Stupid Kentucky and their winning the lottery instead of us," Emily returned. "All right, I need to go print something. I'll see you in a minute."

Emily turned to head to her room, and I went into mine to set down my things. I grabbed a Dr. Pepper from the fridge in the lounge and then headed to Josh's room. I had everything ready for my students since they were doing practice problems on gas pressure calculations today.

Everyone was already in Josh's room. Emily, Josh, Darnell, Diane, Mary, David and Christina were all there. I was the last one to arrive. Mary was wearing a t-shirt that had all of the chemical ingredients in an "all natural" banana listed. After I entered Josh locked his door and made sure that it was closed. It felt weird and again I didn't know what to make of it.

"Hey everyone, sorry about the awkwardness of all of this but I had to get all of us together since this can't leave the room," Josh started saying to us. "Why don't we all sit down over here so no one can hear us." He motioned for us to sit in a circle by the board away from the door. We all sat down quickly as our curiosity was now immense. Josh smiled a huge goofy grin. "We won," he said. Then he paused as if he expected us to join him in smiling. I sarcastically gave David a high five.

"Won what?" Darnell asked.

"We won...." Josh replied. "We won the lottery. 1.8 billion dollars, it's ours."

"No we didn't," said Christina. "The only winning ticket was sold in Kentucky."

"I know," said Josh. "That was our ticket. I hurt my neck yesterday and was complaining about having to go out and buy lottery tickets for us when I was talking to my Dad who lives in Kentucky. He offered to go buy them for me and so I told him if he did and we won that I'd give him a million dollars of it. It's our ticket, we won."

"Okay...." I said.

"Look, here's a picture of the ticket from last night from my Dad along with our agreement," Josh switched to convincing us. "He sent me another picture along with the receipt this morning too. Check the numbers if you don't believe it."

David looked on his phone. "Those are the winning numbers," he said quietly. "We won?"

"We won," Josh said again with the biggest grin you've ever seen.

No one said anything for a minute. It took a minute for the reality to set in. We weren't believing 100% just yet; this could still be an elaborate prank. But the possibility was now real and our belief was building. Before we could obtain that certainty either way our minds started to wander. What would this do for the rest of our lives? Would we never see each other anymore? Would we all quit? Would we all move away into mansions in other states? And then we started to shift into the practical part. Would we quit today? Could we go back to sleep right now? Did we need security? How long would it take to get the money?

"So listen," Josh finally continued as our heads raced. "I know this is a lot to take in because and I thought a lot about this all night. I think that a lot of big changes are going to happen and I'm super pumped. But, I'm worried about changing all of our lives so suddenly. I don't know if everyone remembers this, but when we drafted our contract for the lottery playing rules, we had some conditions."

"You're kidding," Emily jumped in. "The one of us needs to be fired before we collect the money rule?" she asked.

"So here's what I've been thinking," Josh responded calmly. "I know it was meant to be stupid at the time, but I think it might actually be really great. I mean, none of us ever need to work again. Each of us will get just under 140 million. But before we all move, or quit, or retire or whatever, think about how much fun we could have for a few weeks if we all follow through on that clause. Think about how great it would be for us to be silly every day, to not have to worry about paperwork, or dressing professionally and we can just come in and do whatever we want. It will be one last hurrah for our group. Working with you has been a huge part of my life, and I can't think of a better way for that to conclude than the eight of us trying as hard as possible to get fired while no one else knows about this."

"Okay," I announced. "I completely agree. I haven't had a lot of friends growing up and a lot of my friends from the past have moved. My life is great right now and I'm not turning down my share or anything, but a couple of weeks of goofing around and trying to get fired sounds amazing. I'm in."

"Me too," Darnell stated and smiled.

"And you shall have my axe," David announced like Gimli from Lord of the Rings.

"And my homework," said Diane with a wink. Her eyes twinkled.

"Yes," agreed Emily. Mary and Christina nodded.

"Great," said Josh. "Let's make sure we're all comfortable with the rules though one last time. The first to get fired gets an extra ten million from each person. So currently the 7 "losers" get 130 million. The first to get fired would win 210 million." We all nodded in agreement.

"Maybe we should all donate a portion to the school for the havoc we're about to unleash," I whispered. Diane smiled partially from excitement about winning and partially about the anticipation.

"Hang on," Josh interrupted. "So the first to get fired gets 210 million. But there are rules. It doesn't count if you ask to get fired or let anyone know outside of us 8. You also can't just do something illegal, insubordinate or downright immoral. It has to be something clever and funny." The whole room was grinning. "Before we start, I know I need everyone to trust me so I will have a lawyer put the money into a trust and draft a contract so there's no worry about me lying or a dispute. I'll get that done today because I'm going to call in sick in a moment to go take care of my daughter. In order for this to work though, we need to keep all of this between us 8. Not even your spouses can know because if they know, they'll screw it up. What do we all say?"

We all nodded and a few chimed in with some verbal agreements. "Cool," said Josh. "In that case I'm going to go get proof of everything settled and hopefully by Monday next week the games can begin. Don't start anything until we get a legal agreement in place"

You would think that we'd burst into screams of joy. Instead we all left the room quietly to go back to our rooms and decompress for a second. It was daunting to think about teaching after this meeting. Our minds were all racing between how our lives were about to change but also coming up with ideas on how we could get fired by doing something funny. I also was really glad that everyone had agreed to stick to the original agreement. This was about to be so much fun in so many different ways. I couldn't wait. I locked the door so no one could come in yet even though class started in seven minutes. I just sat and put my head down and smiled. After a minute I got back up from my seat and did a jump with a heel click on my way back to unlock the door. The students quickly piled into my room and sat down.

"Hey Mr. Miles," shouted Sydney. "Why the locked door?"

"Sorry, I had to think for a second," I responded.

"What was the occasion?" smirked Matt.

"Hilarious," I snarked back. "Want to hear a joke Matt? What rhymes with Matt has Saturday detention?" Matt shrugged. "Matt has Sunday detention," I concluded.

"I can't have detention on Sunday," Matt replied. "I'll be way too busy learning chemistry all day."

I started to relax. It was crazy that even with such big news, I could still quickly transition back into the rush of the teaching day. I looked forward to lunch so we could talk some more, but I had student questions for the bulk of the first three hours and somehow concern over their grades displaced concern over the rest of my life. When I finally got to lunch, I was exhausted. I locked my classroom door and briskly walked down to the lounge. But to my great disappointment, there were already two other teachers not in our group and a substitute eating lunch. I tried to hide my reaction as I realized we weren't going to be able to discuss this out in the open at all. Diane came in shortly after me and gave me a look like she also wished that we had lunch with just the eight of us. After some awkward small talk, I thought about heading back to my class. The sub was asking if he should check with the office before leaving if they have prep during the last class of the day, and I just did not care at all. Someone else started explaining what to do, and I just stood up and mumbled something about being busy and went back to my room. There was still 14 minutes before 4th hour started. Diane walked into my room right after I got there.

"Hey, I think we should head out to the bar after school today," Diane said.

"Yeah, I agree," I responded. "Lots to talk about. In fact, let's go to my house as many of us that can make it and have a drink and get our heads on straight about all of this."

"Sounds good," Diane said. "I'll invite everyone else if you can tell Josh about it."

"Got it," I said. I started texting him right that instant before students would get back from lunch.

When the final class was over, I barely could wait long enough to let the last student out of the class. I had never realized that some students took an agonizingly long time to pack their bags and leave. After a very long two minutes, I locked up and drove to the store quickly to pick up some drinks and then home. Emily and Darnell were already there and Diane was en route after also stopping by to give the cross-country team a practice itinerary.

We sat down and opened some drinks to celebrate. "Josh said he can't make it because he has to make arrangements still, but to enjoy one for him," I told everyone.

"I don't know what to make of all of this, it still feels surreal," Darnell said. Mary walked in and proceeded to do a celebratory dirty bird dance.

"I have so many ideas for how to get fired," Mary informed us. She was wearing a shirt that said "Just as I thought, you're basic" and had a pink phenolphthalein solution. "I think that I might be more excited about the next week of school than I am about being rich."

"I thought of a couple too," Darnell smirked. Soon everyone but Josh had arrived and we were having a great time without revealing our ideas to each other.

"We should also do some things just for fun that we've always wanted to do," David told us. "I think we should reply to every email from parents and students by just saying 'I don't understand what it is you want' regardless of what the email says."

"I have a few that would be perfect for that," Christine laughed.

"Have you thought about how you're going to surprise your spouses?" Emily asked.

"At first I was worried about keeping this a secret," I explained, "but if our spouses all know it's going to mess up everything else and I'm pretty confident my wife will forgive when she finds out we have two hundred ten million dollars and she won't need an alarm clock for the rest of her life."

"You mean one hundred thirty million?" David asked me.

"Nope, I was right the first time," I responded confidently.

"We shall see," Diane replied. "I think you underestimate how much pent up aggression I am about to unfold next week."

"I think we should talk about something else too," Christine interrupted us. "We're going to be screwing over Donna and the rest of the school big time here. I mean that's going to be eight of us quitting at once and we're going to unleash some terror on the school before we do. I'm thinking it might be good if we all agree to put some money towards the school. That way they'll be able to put up a signing bonus and be able to hire someone."

"We should throw a big party too, and I agree about making a donation," David said. We spent about another hour trash talking each other about the ruckus we were about to unload and thinking through what we would buy and how our lives would soon change. We still had a lot of thoughts rushing through, but really, we couldn't wrap our heads around things completely until we found out the full details from Josh later. After another hour we split up to pick up kids from school, run some errands, head home and enjoy normal life for a little bit longer.

Josh sent out a group message that we would meet tomorrow after school and that he would be out all day, but he should be ready by then. I told everyone we would meet at my house again but then avoid it after that so we didn't raise suspicions.

The school day was interesting. It felt like a mostly normal day but when I got an email complaint from a parent it felt different. I couldn't take anything personally at the moment. Even though the complaint was from a parent whose kid was currently putting out the most marginal of efforts in class, it was far too unimportant to have any impact on me. At lunch we still had normal conversation, although I noticed that many of us had gone out to restaurants the night before and were eating leftovers. Diane had prime rib with asparagus and those little potatoes with a slightly burned skin. I had deep dish pepperoni pizza, and David had brought in ribs. There were other teachers eating with us today, so we were muted aside from some darting glances. Midway through lunch Emily finally arrived with an apple pie with crumb topping.

After school I again had to wait about two full minutes for the last student to get out before speed walking to my car and battling the after school traffic. I had sent a message to our team captain during school so we could all get out as quickly as possible. Since there were no stops at the store this time, I arrived second, but three cars were there before I got inside. Josh had been waiting since he had called off sick. Within three more minutes, all eight of us were inside.

"I brought contracts to sign," Josh started telling us. "This confirms the amount paid once one of us gets fired and also includes the rules for what counts for getting fired and what does not. The winner gets an additional share of the money and nobody gets paid until someone does get fired. If someone goes too far and gets arrested or fired while violating the rules then the money will stay until someone gets fired legitimately. The money is already transferring now to an account where it will be stored until we split it amongst ourselves. However, I figured for fun, and in case it takes a couple of weeks, that I would take ten thousand out for each of us for a little bit of spending money to tide us over. I'll get it in cash so you can do what you want with it, but keep it discrete. If you tell anyone outside of us eight or the lawyer, there are penalties. And that includes family. The exception is that my dad obviously knows already, so I have made a conditional payment to him upon his discretion lasting throughout the process. What questions do we have?"

"When do we start?" Mary asked.

"As soon as we have all eight signed," Josh replied. We signed the contract and agreed that tomorrow would kick things off. We also agreed that we would chip in some money from all of us to make amends with the school afterwards. After that we headed home to start making plans towards creative means to have some fun and hopefully get terminated from teaching. I had to take advantage of using my Twitter account and YouTube channel, but I really longed to do something with the PA system. The first thing I did was to call in sick though.

70

Chapter 5 Day of Chaos

The next day I got to work a bit early. On my way into the school, there was a car parked in front of the main entrance. By in front of the main entrance, I mean they were less than foot away from the door. As I approached the car, I realized it was jacked up off of the ground and it was Josh's old car. The hood was up and the flashers were blinking. I continued into the office. The school secretary asked if I was setting up my room before heading back home for the day. "Something like that," I replied. She told me she hoped that no one was sick at my house. I assured her everything was fine, just some school business to take care of and I needed the day to straighten everything out. I headed upstairs and unpacked my first day of stuff. I locked the room and got everything ready.

When the sub arrived, he opened the door and came in. I told him that I was going to be teaching part of the day but needed him to watch the class during specific parts of hours while I was in and out and that I would handle the lessons. It was about twenty minutes before school when all of a sudden, the PA system kicked on. It was David and he had snuck into the office and hid the PA machine in the closet of the office. He started making phone noises and beeping sounds, then tried to answer the office phone. I giggled a little bit, but the longer it went on the funnier it got. He started ranking his top five favorite tacos of all time and I lost it a little bit. Then all of a sudden, I heard a door, Donna yelled, "What are you doing?"

and the PA system shut off. I went into the supply room to laugh for a bit and Diane came in.

"I locked my door," she told me while smiling.

"Ok....." I said confused about why that was relevant. It turns out she intended to just sit in her room playing computer games with the door locked as long as possible. She made it eleven minutes into first hour before someone went to the office where they keyed into her room. I saw Donna heading towards her room so I ran to the supply room to eavesdrop.

"Why didn't you open the door Diane?" Donna asked.

"Oh, sorry, I guess I lost track of time and thought it was an hour earlier, you know how the time change messes us up," Diane replied quickly.

"The time change isn't for two more months," Donna expressed incredulously.

"Exactly," Diane responded while nodding seriously. I had to cover my mouth to not blow my cover by laughing too loudly. I retreated to my room and spent a minute cracking up. At this point I had not given the students any instruction on what to do and the sub seemed very confused. I told him I would be back in just a minute and that something had come up. I took my bag down to the lounge and in the bathroom filled up water balloons for about fifteen minutes. When I got back to class, I had a bag full of them that I hid in a backpack so my secret would last until the appropriate time. I took attendance and reminded students that we had a test coming up soon and that they had better be making good use of their time. They looked around confused because we most certainly did not have a test coming up soon but the sub seemed content and started to read a book. Then I took the water balloons into the hallway and threw one at a kid heading back to class from the bathroom.

"What the hell?" the kid exclaimed and he ran back to Josh's room. I ran after him and interrupted Josh's class.

"Don't ever swear at me again or you'll be suspended," I yelled at the kid then threw another water balloon at the back wall and ran. When I got back to class the bell rang and first hour left. The sub asked if there was something they were supposed to be working on when I was gone. I mumbled about reviewing and went to go find out what happened to Diane.

Next hour was the student announcements and it was a gem. The two students introduced themselves and started talking about where clubs meet and results from sports. Then all of a sudden, the one says, "I like big butts and I cannot lie. You other brothers can't deny. When a girl walks in with an itty-bitty waist and a round thing in your face you get clubbed. Join the big butts club, for those interested see Mr. Fields in the main office after school on Tuesdays in room 306. Food will be provided."

I died laughing. I moved into the supply room and Diane walked in with a smile on her face. "Did you see my announcement?" she asked me.

"That was you?" I asked. "That was incredible. Is Mr. Fields going to know it was you?"

"He might find out soon," she said and then winked. We both laughed for a minute and headed back to our classes. When I walked back in a student asked me what we were talking about in the supply room. I thought for a moment instead of responding like I normally would. I decided to go for it and I walked over to my bag and grabbed a water balloon and launched it at the student's feet. The room was stunned and silent.

"Anyone else have any questions?" I announced more than asked. The room was silent and was not sure what to think. Normally they would have thought it was a joke, but I sold the attitude just right and they were mildly terrified. The substitute looked up from his reading but then pretended like he hadn't seen anything and continued with his book. The students quietly got out work to do and worked on stuff from another class. I took my bag out into the hallway to see if any students were taking mid class runs to the bathroom. I saw no one but I heard something weird happening in Darnell's class. When I peeked in through the doorway, I noticed he was not wearing a tie for the first time.

There was some shouting and a weird noise. As I got closer, I had to hide from view so I could laugh. Darnell was using a blender as he taught. Every time he started to talk, he started the blender. A student raised her hand and started to ask him to go back a slide when he interrupted with the blender while shouting, "WHAT? I CAN'T HEAR YOU!" As the blender noise dropped, the girl tried to ask her question again but the blender started right back up. The students looked extremely confused. It was genius. I figured I would add to the chaos and I peeked my head in, then went back into the hallway and got out a water balloon. "IT'S HARD TO HEAR YOUR QUESTION OVER THE BLENDER!" he yelled again.

I waited until he started the blender again and then I ran in shouting, "Blender distraction attack!!!!" I launched a balloon at the corner of the room where it hit the desk of two students. I paused like I was confused, then I pulled out a second balloon and threw it to the other corner where a girl ducked at the last second for it to miss hitting her in the face.

The entire scene was epic because Darnell didn't miss a beat on the blender. He kept running it at high speed and shouted things like, "WATER BALLOON WHAT?" I dropped to the floor and I army crawled out of the room. On my way back there was a student walking to the bathroom while texting on their phone.

"Do you have a pass?" I inquired in a slightly louder tone than normal.

The student looked up after a second had passed. "What?" they asked.

"Do you have a pass?" I asked with the exact same timing and tone as before.

"Oh, yeah, it's this bucket that Mrs. Chase uses," the student explained and then continued to not pay attention to me. They got a water balloon exploding at their shoes for their lack of attention as I ducked back into my classroom before I could hear how they reacted. Luckily the bell rang right as I entered and the class quietly got up and left.

The next hour that came in seemed somewhat cautious as they entered. They must have been forewarned somehow. I left the room to go walk around and see what everyone else was doing. I was not disappointed. I walked into Josh's room just as the bell was ringing. Josh was funny with his students and had really strong relationships. So when he started jumping around to hype them up they mostly went along with it. "Are you ready to learn?" he asked loudly. Then he moved to the other side of the room. "I said, are you ready to learn?"

"Yes," one student said while smiling at the front of the room.

"No, no, no," Josh continued. "I need to know that all of you are ready to learn. Are you ready to learn?" A few more students said yes and the enthusiasm picked up a little bit. "No, no, no. I want to hear you shout it, ARE YOU READY TO LEARN?" Josh exclaimed.

"Yes," several students shouted lightly.

"Let's go!" Josh shouted. Then he hit play on a boombox and warm up music they play before basketball games started playing loudly. "It's learning time," he shouted again and this time ripped off his pants. He had been wearing tearaway pants the whole time. If I hadn't been in front of a class of students I might have peed. Underneath he was wearing short mesh basketball shorts and he ran around the room giving high fives to his students with his hairy legs hanging out. I stayed for a few minutes and found out this wasn't just an introduction to the class. Later he asked the class, "I said, what is the y-intercept?"

"Zero," one of the students at the front yelled out.

"ZERO!" Josh exclaimed and again ripped off his tearaway pants and did a lap around the class with music blaring. Every time he got done doing a lap, he buttoned them back up to rip them off again in a few minutes. I got a drink on my way back to my class so I could get composed. When I got back, I told the sub I was leaving to go get some lunch. I think he was completely terrified of me at this point, so he didn't ask any questions and just nodded politely. I went out and grabbed some fried chicken and brought it back just in time to eat. We were all in the room within about ten seconds of the bell ringing and we were howling with laughter.

"Scott, you have no idea how perfectly timed your water balloon was," Josh informed me. "This kid had been the only one to yell out yes when I asked if they were ready to learn and then the water balloon flew against the wall and then I ripped off my tearaways."

"Where did you even get those things?" Christine asked while laughing.

"Middle school," Josh shrugged.

"And they still fit?" Emily asked incredulously.

"Well I don't wear them regularly if that's what you're wondering," Josh reassured everyone. "But I've been hoping to wear them as a joke for years now and today was the perfect opportunity."

"What happened when you got caught?" Diane asked David.

David started talking and was clearly embarrassed, "Oh my goodness it was so awkward. Donna was behind Maurice and they both were just staring at me like I was a moron. I didn't know what to say so I finally told them I got confused and then walked away."

"Josh, why is your car parked at the front entrance?" Christine inquired.

"I think something is wrong with it, not sure exactly," he replied innocently.

"Did you get a flat tire and disconnect the battery after moving the car to a highly inconvenient location?" David suggested.

"Did Donna get a glimpse of your hairy legs when she stopped by your class to listen to you stumble through an idiotic explanation of the situation?" I asked.

"My legs are beautiful," Josh defended himself.

"I made $117 today," Christine announced as she passed around a note. The note read:

English is not a blow off class. To verify this I will be collecting bribes today and tomorrow only. Every dollar will result in one point being added to your grade. Cash only!

"Ok, so as great as this is, and today might be the best day of my life since the days that my kids were born," Emily started telling us as the note finished its way around the table, "I think we might need to revise this somehow. We're going to make life a living hell for Donna and probably the custodians as well. Can we come up with a way to make this slightly more controlled?"

"I was thinking the same thing," Diane said.

"I bet that you were, given what you put Eric through today," I laughed and then gave Diane a fist bump.

"Worth it," she replied. "But I'm not sure it will be worth it with all eight of us going hard for a longer period of time."

"I had a similar thought," Mary started to explain. "And here's an idea I had. What if instead of all eight of us doing crazy things for the next few days, we grouped up into teams of four and made plans where one person does something crazy. Then the first team that has their person get fired wins and they split the money between the four of them." Mary was serious in spite of wearing a bathrobe with dinosaur slippers. The dinosaurs made small roaring noises when she walked.

"That sounds great to me," I said. "I think it would keep things fun, have plenty of incentive, but also I'm having a hard time thinking of things that will actually get me fired without crossing the line too far. It'd also put less strain on Donna than having eight of her friends go nuts in the same day."

"Water balloons was a pretty weak idea," David told me.

"I thought it would be epic when I went through with it," I responded. "But so far it's been more weird than awesome."

"So, in terms of revising the deal I can revise the contracts to split the money differently as long as all eight of us agree to it," Josh informed us. "I asked the lawyers about this exact scenario when we were drafting the papers and it's not too difficult to change."

"Is anyone opposed or do we all mostly agree with changing it up?" David asked the group.

"I would like to change it, but I feel better doing so after school where we can speak freely a bit more. It's nice we're the only eight at lunch today but it'd be better if we had a bit more privacy to selecting teams and working out the little details," Emily said. We all agreed with her and everyone was into the idea of doing some revisions now that we had tried this out for a half of a day.

"Oh geez, I don't know how to do the rest of the day now," Emily complained. "I'd been teaching the kids swear words in Spanish but telling them they were other things instead."

"You did not!" I shouted. "That's amazing."

Emily laughed and said, "It's the dream of every Spanish teacher, I think. One kid said in Spanish that he ate shit in his kitchen and I nearly died laughing."

"Scott, did you get a sub today?" Mary asked me.

"Maybe...." I replied sheepishly. "Is that cheating?" I asked.

"If you have a sub, come to one of my next two classes," Diane instructed me. "We've been doing blindfolded races in the hallway in a single elimination format."

"No that's brilliant," Josh said somehow not noticing what Diane had just said. "Too bad I'll be fired for too many sick days if I grab one Monday or I'd do it too. We should try and rotate subs around between us so we all can use one if needed but we don't take too many days in a row."

"Sounds good, we'll hash out the rest after school at Scott's place I assume," Darnell added.

"Yep, my place as soon as we can get there," I confirmed.

***

With a sub in my room I left early to beat the traffic. I also wanted to write down all of the things everyone had done today and make a little journal to remember everything by. I figured we'd all be separating soon and this would make a great way to remember our last time together at school. I also started a new document with what we needed to accomplish at our meeting. We would need to choose teams, revise our contracts, sign everything and then probably meet with our team and make some plans. Josh and David arrived first and both had brought drinks with them. We sat out on the deck while waiting for the others. Diane got there last about seven minutes later.

"Sorry," I had to get practice rolling," she said. "I just had them run two miles easy and then go home." I had completely forgotten about practice so I was glad someone was still adulting today.

"Sorry Diane, I completely forgot about practice with all of the chaos going on," I apologized.

"No worries, maybe we'll alternate days for a bit so we don't tank the team, but start transitioning out as well," she proposed.

"Sounds good. By the way, that announcement was bold and fantastic this morning," I replied.

"Why thank you," she said and smiled.

"Ok, I missed the announcement," Darnell announced. "What was it?"

"It was awesome," David explained. "The kid reading the announcements did the first verse of Baby Got Back and then announced a Big Butts Club meeting in the assistant principal's office after school on Tuesdays."

"You didn't!" Darnell stated.

"Oh, but I did," Diane concluded. "I was two for two on the day," she bragged.

"I heard Donna come talk to you," I said excitedly. "When you blamed it on the time change and she said that the time change wasn't for another few weeks and you just said exactly, I lost it." Diane smiled and was clearly pleased with her day one efforts.

Josh interrupted our reminiscing from our lovely day of pranks. "Since we're all here and before anyone has too much to drink for this to be street legal, is everyone agreed about forming teams and splitting the money amongst the winning team of four?"

"I like four better, but I'd be fine with teams of two as well," Mary responded.

"I agree, four is preferred, but I want to do teams as long as no one opposes," David added. We all agreed on teams and no one wanted to do teams of two.

"Next we need to pick teams and we should plan out how to do this so no one feels like it's unfair," Josh directed.

"I say team captains!" I announced.

"Who will the captains be?" Diane asked.

Darnell quickly chimed in, "I think Scott and Diane should be captains with Scott choosing first since Diane clearly is ahead."

"Agreed," Mary and Emily said at the same time.

"That's fine with me," I said. "But I'd want to do alternating picks so that it's fair."

"What do you mean alternating picks?" Josh asked.

"I'd pick first, then Diane would pick second and third, then I would pick fourth and fifth, she would get sixth and seventh and I would choose last," I explained.

"You'd only need six picks since two of you are already captains," David corrected me.

"Are we sure we trust Scott to not screw this up?" Josh asked.

"Yes, as long as I don't end up on his team," Darnell assured Josh. Everyone else agreed, regardless of team placement. So we started splitting up into teams.

"With the first pick of the draft, Team Scott Miles selects Josh," I announced like a commissioner on draft night. Diane picked David and Darnell. I chose Emily and Christina and Mary went with Diane. "I would have picked you Mary, but I figured you'd want to be with your bestie Diane," I said. Josh had already been working on getting new contracts and he would pick them up tonight and bring them to school tomorrow where we would restart. Hopefully no one would get fired overnight or things would get complicated. Then we split off and Diane's team went to go drive to get ice cream and brainstorm ideas. Josh, Emily, Christina and I started thinking in my living room and coming up with a schedule and some objectives.

"Ok, I'm just going to throw this out there and see how people react to it," I started. "I'm thinking we should make an actual cannon."

"We can't get fired for using a cannon, it would violate the no weapons rule," Emily ruled it out.

"Is a cannon a weapon?" I asked. "I mean, if it's not firing cannonballs but instead is firing fast food or textbooks or something?"

"We'll keep that as a plan C," Josh said diplomatically. "So which of us four is most likely to get fired if only one of us is going to carry out the plans?"

"Probably me," I suggested. "We all have tenure and I'm the most willing to do something breathtakingly stupid."

"But you teach chemistry, they'll never be able to replace you," Christine disagreed.

"They can't replace any teachers at the moment," Josh replied. "Let's start with trying to get Scott fired. He's got the biggest rap sheet with Donna for starters and I'm confident in him being a complete idiot."

"Thank you," I responded and wiped away a small tear from my eye.

"Let's start profiling Scott, then to get some ideas," Josh continued. "Chemistry teacher, so we have chemicals to use. Do you think that you can fill up the hallway with smoke?"

"I'll start thinking of some pranks I could pull," I started thinking through my inventory and writing down some thoughts.

"I think it would be smart to prank Diane," Emily suggested. "That might make Donna feel bad for her and make her less likely to get fired."

"That's smart, but we need to think of something awesome that will really get Scott in trouble and not just make her laugh," Josh recommended. "Are you still making that YouTube channel stuff?"

"Yeah!" I exclaimed. I had barely even thought of using my social media presence, but that opened up a lot of ideas for me that I had always wanted to do. "I have some ideas but let me put together some official thoughts on that tonight after our meeting," I added.

"I think we should do more than one thing; maybe we could also do an email blitz every day after school or at lunch where we craft responses to emails and maybe send some reply all," Christine added.

"That's great, I can start putting together some generic drafts of things that I'd like to say to parents as well as some super weird emails to just send off whenever," Emily contributed. "I mean, I want to do things that are funny, but it also has to be possible to get fired from. They aren't going to fire us for making funny noises over the PA. The best way would be to piss off some parents or someone from the central office administration. But we need to make sure it's clever and creative at the same time."

"We also need to keep Diane employed," Josh circled back. "She's already gotten a bit of a head start today and she's got some creativity on her side as well. She's a physics teacher and a head coach, so she has a lot of chances to do something and she's bold. Scott are you sure you can beat her?"

"Honestly, no, but I'll go down swinging either way," I offered. Diane was very smart and clever and I would not be surprised to see her doing something extremely creative. I think she was already on Donna and Eric's bad sides. "Let's come up with some more strategy. What have you always wanted to do as a teacher but wouldn't do because it would make you look bad and lead to discipline?" I asked.

"Email responses is high on my list," Emily said. "Probably being a little bit more honest with students without being overly harsh too."

"What about making a list of students you like and don't like," Christine offered.

"A ranking system," Josh added on.

"What else besides students annoys you though?" I asked. I wanted a lot of options to choose from and we could start planning once we had a substantial brainstorm.

"Well grading sucks, meetings are terrible and the goals we have to write are obnoxious for starters," Josh summarized.

"When's our next staff meeting?" I asked.

"It should be Wednesday next week," Emily responded.

"I should do something at the meeting," I whispered.

"I've always wanted that poster that says the beatings will continue until morale improves," Emily offered. "Maybe we could start by making new posters for your room that are demotivational but also go too far and are out of line."

"We should target specific students in official posters," Christine exclaimed.

"Yes!" I agreed. "I have many students that should have a poster made about them. I wonder if I could sneak a picture of them in class sleeping or something and put together a poster from that picture."

"That'd be amazing," Josh agreed. "I'll call a print shop and find out what they need and how quickly we'd be able to get them." Josh went into the other room and called some places on his phone.

"Well I wasn't planning on grading anything ever again but I do recall seeing stickers that made fun of the crappy parts of student work on my twitter feed," I remarked.

"I'll see what I can find for stickers for grading," Christine declared. "Maybe we'll need to bundle that with our poster production." She started searching for sticker ideas online and also for places that could print stickers for us. I compiled a list of ideas and when we could put everything together. Emily and I figured we could meet as a group at lunch every day and work out any emails that could be returned, reply all emails we could send, room decorations and upcoming school functions. We'd also have to be on the lookout for options to utilize Diane's ideas against her and for any special situations like the upcoming staff meeting and Homecoming dance.

The print shop said they could make a laminated poster from any picture along with added text in about an hour and the pricing was cheaper than we thought. Josh and Emily decided they would design a few and we would go over them Monday together, choose a couple and take the pictures needed to make them after school. I was going to work on creating a top ten and bottom ten students list to post for my classes along with the reasons why the bottom ten weren't cutting it. Christine was going to make fun grading stickers to put on returned assignments and quizzes. Then we decided we would meet daily at the beginning of lunch to come up with email responses as a group except on Thursdays when we would continue doing our group lunches where we all brought something in. But we still needed something big to really tie everything together. We couldn't think of it but we agreed we would start working on everything and when someone caught an idea we'd share it via email.

Everyone packed up to go work on their assignments and I picked up the kids from school. When we got back I told my family I had to grade some stuff and instead starting going through my student lists to come up with my top ten and bottom ten students. I figured if I could pick most of the top ten from one class it would make the list even more controversial and awkward. As I opened up the internet browser, I had a thought. I sent everyone an email.

Dear Team Scott Miles,
I have an idea for something we could do. I have my YouTube channel running mostly on gaming for Xbox right now but I used to make chemistry videos. What if I made a set of YouTube videos called "Chemistry with Jesus" where I dress up like Jesus and then teach chemistry with a bunch of biblical puns worked in. In the description we'll refer to me as White

Jesus. If it goes well maybe we could do a video at lunch in two days and afterwards I could go break some bread in the cafeteria.

I quickly got a reply from Josh.

I love it, I think I can get a costume for it by Tuesday if you work out the script.
Josh

I put a pause on the top ten and bottom ten lists and started coming up with ideas that would be hilarious and mildly controversial perhaps. I figured the introduction could start by saying something along the lines of "Your chemistry prayers are answered" and then I would appear and start teaching chemistry. Maybe "Do you love Jesus but hate chemistry?" would work better. I started a running list of potential introductions:
Your chemistry prayers are answered!
Do you love Jesus but hate chemistry?
Jesus loves you, Chemistry hates you
Jesus loves you, chemistry not so much
White Jesus and the parable of chemistry
Jesus, Chemistry and you need a miracle
What Would Chemistry Jesus Do (WWCJD)?
Jesus Christ Chem Super Star
Jesus take the Beaker

Then I wondered about if I should just teach chemistry oblivious to the fact that I dressed as Jesus or if I should try and work in some puns. We were about to learn about specific heat capacity and I was definitely going to assign the video as homework for points. I settled on writing questions that were related to biblical scriptures. I also figured I would use some flash cotton and then I'd do a bit of video editing to make the answer appear without me working it out. I felt slightly dirty about the whole thing but the bonus money kept me going. I put together some slides to work off of and figured I could do the rest once we had a costume. It was getting late so I put aside my work and read to the kids before they went to bed.

Chapter 6 Lesson Plans

Emily had taken Monday off to get us a sub so I didn't have to torture a person two school days in a row. I sat at my desk and worked on making a script for the video. I also came up with an assignment I could put grades on, a list of things students did that I found irritating and pranks to do to Diane. I figured that today would be a day of preparation and making sure that our plans worked well and tomorrow the fun would start over again. My second hour was still nervous, so I tried to act a little bit kinder and normal towards them. I had the classes write an explanation of why they thought it felt most comfortable when the room temperature was seventy degrees instead of the same temperature as their bodies. Then after about twenty-five minutes they had to take turns explaining what they understand and what they do not understand before coming up with two lingering questions.

My students were not very irritating this year, but the few incidents that had happened brought back memories of wrongs from the past. I had several things that I typically overlooked for my own mental health, but how hard is it to pick up your trash and water bottle at the end of class? Another obnoxious thing was some students would write on the lab desks in pencil because they figured it would just erase. I also had a student named Fred in third hour that used to shoot staples from the stapler. I had been warned about Fred from Mary, but he had mostly been ok in my class besides being annoying at times. I had a group of three that did that stupid bottle flipping and one more that took really long to sit down even though she came in to class right as the bell was ringing. Before lunch I realized I was going to have to rotate the bottom ten. I would start with my students that would call out sick for appointments during tests though.

I also had an easy time putting together the top ten. I had students that thought hard about science. I had students that had given me really nice compliments. Two students had written me a postcard as an assignment for another class. One student would push in chairs after class and that is the best way to show what a great student you are. I also had one student in my sixth hour that had a hard time but worked so hard and did everything I suggested with incredible attention to detail and tremendous effort. I had great artists, funny students and all kinds of students that were great students. I printed out some seating charts so I could cut out the students' photos to put into a poster. A couple were just really funny and smart and were a pleasure to teach.

I started cutting out the photos of students to put together my initial top and bottom ten as the bell rang for lunch. Diane popped her head in briefly to let me know that she and her team were also meeting for lunch but they also figured we would still spend Thursdays together as a group to celebrate the fun and make sure the competition didn't end up dividing us in any way. As she was leaving Josh walked in and made a comment about her not stealing our ideas.

Emily and Christine walked in behind Josh and we started talking about emails while I continued to organize photos and rank the students. I figured it would be most controversial if I actually put them in order where one student got the ranking of bottom student and then the 2nd worst and so on instead of just a pile of ten students all at the bottom. Christine agreed that would be more controversial.

I had not received any emails since we won, but Josh had gotten an inquiry about his tearaway pants and Christine had gotten a question about improving a student's grade in the school newspaper class. "They literally get an A just for doing their writing assignments," Christine vented. "What the hell am I supposed to say about how to do better?"

"May I?" Josh asked and gestured towards her laptop. Christine nodded and Josh began typing.

I feel it has been made abundantly clear how the grading works in this class and so I am not sure if this email is meant to challenge the grading system in my class or if it is just to try and make me feel bad for the mistakes your child has made. Please clarify if I am missing something.
Thanks,
Dr. Gardner

Josh then handed the computer to Christine who changed the comma after thanks to an exclamation point and then hit send. "This is the best feeling in the world," she exclaimed. "I've wanted to hit send on one of these forever and that child has done nothing to warrant effort on my behalf to improve his grade. Normally I type that out and then don't send it and just save the draft."

"So what should I send about the tearaway pants?" Josh asked us. I took a turn with the email drafting.

Uh, you're welcome…. ;)

Josh fell off of his chair laughing. Then he hit send. "I know we're targeting Miles getting fired but these emails might end up with a meeting with human resources as well," Josh laughed.

"Has anyone heard or seen anything from Diane's team yet?" Emily asked.

"No, but I think they're doing the same thing we are and spending a day to plan," I answered. "As much as I would like to win, I am looking forward to what they come up with." Diane and I had also agreed to alternate practices with the team and I chose to start so that I only missed time during the planning day. I finished ranking my students and the four of us made a very nice-looking poster with emojis.

Josh admired our work. "I made arrangements for your costume by the way; it should be ready tomorrow."

Emily added, "I can handle the makeup component too, I have some plans."

"I think I have the script mostly worked out, although usually I just start talking and go from there,"

I explained. "I have a few ideas but at worst I'll just need to tape a couple of times and do some minor editing after."

"We should meet this weekend to work on some ideas for next week too," Christine added. "Let's meet at the bar on Saturday."

"Actually, my family is on a trip, so let's meet at my house," said Josh. "That way we can be a bit more free with what we say. I'm worried about talking about this in public still."

"Sounds great," I confirmed. "I'll film the video tomorrow, edit it and publish by bedtime. Then I can assign it to the students to watch as a flipped learning homework assignment."

Next we looked over the three poster drafts.

Are your grades too low?

Maybe try lining up at the door 3 minutes before class ends!

Only A students can work on homework from another class

PS the A stands for @sshole

**If you're too stupid to wear goggles
in chem lab, the Ivy League might
be just out of your reach!**

"Did they not have a goggles shape?" Josh asked.

"I really like the one about the Ivy League school," I commented. "I think we should put ambiguous pictures of actual students on them as well. I'll try sneaking a few photos that we can edit for them next hour."

"I like all of them and don't think it will be a big hassle for us to spring for three posters," Josh responded. "Let's all take some photos of students in our classes. Especially if they're doing anything annoying. I'm going to order some prints for my room as well."

Christine had designed some grading stickers over the weekend and we agreed to all start using them.

This is the worst thing that has happened in any school ever

Did you even try a little bit???

This is so bad that it makes the next assignment look better

This is fantastic, especially for you

"These are great but is it worth it to use them to have to grade more stuff?" I pondered.

"I think it will be fine," Emily responded. "I mean, you don't have to critically read everything, just look for some fun spots to put these and then just put in whatever grade you want without putting a typical effort into it. You can do a completion grade and still put the stickers."

"I think the students are going to like these and no one will complain about them, but I still feel great about using them," Christine added. "I'll get them printed and we can all collect something to put them on in the next two days. We also need to think of something Scott can do at the staff meeting in two days."

"Yes, I'm going to be working on the video tomorrow so any ideas would be helpful," I said. "I'll leave that up to you three for now." The end of lunch was approaching so we ate and chatted for a bit. It was nice to have a few minutes to appreciate the brilliance of the whole thing and none of us really cared if we were a few minutes late to start next hour anyways.

***

As everyone was leaving, we saw Donna walking through the hallway with a couple of visitors. I closed my door and walked towards the front of the room to start the students on their assignment. As I moved, the door opened and Donna and her visitor walked in. But it wasn't just a visitor, she had brought the superintendent with her. Our superintendent was tall and had an angry look on her face even when she smiled. She was intimidating but had a reputation for being very kind and helpful. I figured she must be watching different classrooms. My mind raced about what I could do to try and move the needle closer to fired with someone so powerful in the room. I also figured there was no way Donna would be taking her to Diane's room with all of the stunts that she had pulled last week. I thought of an idea, but it was really stupid.

"Eh, what the hell," I thought. "They're after me!" I suddenly shouted in a panicked voice, and I ran to the front of the room while my class looked on in surprise. I dove head first with my arms outstretched. I landed in front of my desk and crawled under as if I were panicked. A few students started to giggle. The seat of my pants was all you could see sticking out into view. Then I started frantically singing Row, Row Row Your Boat. After a round I shouted, "This is terrifying" and "My life is fine" and "Are they still here?" The giggling had stopped and I slowly quieted down without stopping my crazy comments. "Why did I even bring legs to school today?" and "This is why I stopped having birthdays" and "Uh oh" followed by a long pause. I imagined the superintendent initially thought I was making a joke to entertain the students, but now desperately wanted to get out of the room. Before they left though, I had one last event that became possible. I didn't have a lot of time to evaluate whether it was a good idea or great one so I just went for it. I ripped a giant fart. I could feel it coming about and I did it. It was loud, it didn't smell good and the class lost it. I heard the door close a second after, and I finally peeked out from behind the desk. They were gone and the students were louder than I had ever heard a class before. It wasn't how I had thought it might turn out, but it was bold and I might have pushed into the lead.

Diane peeked in through the store room window. I walked over. "What just happened?" she asked me. "I've never heard your class get so loud."

"The superintendent came in and so I jumped under the desk to hide, shouted a bunch of crazy stuff, sang a song and then at the last minute I farted really loudly." Diane bust out laughing and had to put her hand on the wall to steady herself.

"You might win at this rate then. We're not doing anything until tomorrow," she explained.

"We were planning to start tomorrow, but when they walked in I felt I had to do something and it escalated into flatulence." Part of me was really glad Diane popped in to see what happened. I wanted to go tell everyone else, but I figured I should wait on going into the hallway until the tour had ended. Diane went back to teaching something in her class, and I stayed for just a minute extra. It really had been a spur of the moment decision and my brain was still working through what I had done. If I weren't trying to get fired, I think I would officially be terrified of getting my class back under control and even with the new direction, I was not really sure what I wanted to do next.

After a minute, I walked back in. The class settled quickly, although still giggling and smiling quite a bit. A few students had to look away to stop themselves from laughing out loud. I walked up to the front of the room and loudly asked, "And what did we learn from this?"

The class didn't know what to make of that and the smiles dropped. Finally, a bold student raised their hand. "Matt?" I motioned to him to respond.

"Don't eat tacos for breakfast?" he responded with hesitancy.

"Yes, that and many other life lessons there," I responded seriously. Then we transitioned back to normal somehow and they worked on their assignment for the rest of the hour. I felt pretty good by the end because I had managed to get into trouble without damaging any students in the process and they seemed pretty happy.

After school I decided to do a longer run with the team. We had been ignoring them a bit over the last few days and I felt good. We did six miles running out three and back three. Then we did four 200-meter sprints to build some fast twitch muscle fiber. A small cool down and all of a sudden, I was free for a couple of days with Diane running practice tomorrow. I went back to my classroom for a little bit to gather some thoughts.

We had spent time planning as a group, but I wanted to do some individual thinking. I got out some paper and started from the abstract. The goal was to do two things. One was to do all of the things I had always wanted to as a teacher but felt restricted not to do. The other was to come up with creative ideas on how to get fired. I made a separate category for the staff meeting on Wednesday because that might be a great way to gain more separation from team Diane.

Things that bothered me as a teacher came flowing out quickly. I didn't like when students were disrespectful to my stuff. When they left trash lying around my room, when they would use my supplies incorrectly and when they were loud and rude coming into class. I hated the stupid goals we had to write for our evaluation. I didn't like that teaching was isolating and that it was so challenging to work with other staff members on things. The red tape was obnoxious. Trying to order a pack of paper clips was a five form chain of busy work that made it not worth it. We all just bought our own stuff. Waking up early was tough and grading was brutal, but I didn't feel like there was anything to be done to protest those. Or at least something to be done that I could think of at the moment.

Students being disrespectful we had our posters planned and our top ten and bottom ten ranking system. I thought I should make a fourth poster that says "Don't mess with my stapler you piece of trash that never learned how to respect other people's things!" and had a picture of a trash can holding a stapler and shooting the staples out of it. I made a little practice drawing so I could see if a more talented artist from our team could do something with it.

I made a note for goals to do some revisions this weekend in our online goal tracking system but I figured that could wait for later since it was likely to not be a big impact. I had been leaving class unsupervised on the regular since we won, so I had more chances to network with and observe other teachers. So I decided to do something about the office supplies. I remembered the meeting when they added the additional three forms for reimbursement or placing orders. The old principal had told us that "research showed that using the new process would result in district savings." Of course it would, it was a giant pain in the ass to order anything so we all spent our own money instead of the district buying our supplies. I remembered how pissed off we all were.

One of the older teachers had even pointed out what the new policy was doing. It was an English teacher, Mrs. Dever, that would always do a great job sticking up for the new teachers that didn't know how to. She was just about to retire, and she used that buildup of quality teaching currency to advocate for the new teachers, and I really appreciated her at the time.

I drove home without coming up with anymore crazy ideas, but on the way, I stopped at the office supply store and bought a lot of stuff. I got markers, scissors, sticky notes, paper clips and anything that teachers might want. I spent a few hundred dollars. Then before school the next day I put it out in the teacher prep room for the building that had all of the big rolls of butcher paper. I then went upstairs to my room and found an old email that had gone out to the staff. I hit reply all and it loaded that it would send to all of the high school staff.

I was awarded a grant recently that allowed me to purchase school supplies for our staff without having to fill out five forms to place a basic order. If you would like some supplies a generous donor gave some money so that teachers could get quality teaching materials without wasting their time on red tape. Everything in the teacher prep room is free for you to take and enjoy being treated as a professional for once.
Sincerely,

Scott Miles

And send! Ahhhhh it felt great. I somehow had not gotten an annoying email since Thursday, so this was my first chance at teacher revenge on email that I got to partake in. I went down to the supply room just to see what reaction I would get and how long it would take. There were already two teachers looking around at things. A math teacher that I didn't know well and one of the ninth-grade history teachers named Mr. Bill.

"A little salty on that email?" Mr. Bill asked me.

"Could you tell?" I smiled back.

"Just a bit," he nodded and smiled as well. "Bet it felt great to send though. The form crap we have to go through is so stupid." We had a little bit of teacher complaining small talk and then I headed back to my room. I had a text message from Emily saying that she thought it was brilliant and she'd work on buying some supplies for tomorrow with her "new grant" from another "generous donor." On my way back to my room, I got my first glimpse of what Diane's team had planned. She had a large turtle the size of a large pizza. It was on a leash with a big sign that said "Do not pet, training to help blind people!" She was very, very slowly walking with the turtle towards her room. "Good to see you giving back so generously," I remarked with a smile as I walked into my room.

She nodded and told me, "Wait until you see the other animals we have planned." I wouldn't have been surprised if she had somehow managed to bring in a unicorn the next day. A small crowd of students surrounding her and slowly shifted towards her room as the turtle progressed forward.

I heard one student whisper to another one, "Wouldn't the blind people want a different animal that's faster?" I shook my head and cracked another smile. Not only was bringing a training pet to school hilarious, the mess the animals might make would easily get Diane into trouble. I wondered if just Diane had brought an animal in or if David, Darnell or Mary had done something too. I headed down to David's room to peak in and find out. He had no animal and was typing on his computer.

"Did she actually walk in here with a turtle?" David asked as I walked into the room.

"She actually brought a turtle. It's pretty big too."

"It's much nicer watching her do the pranks and goofy things than making a fool of myself," he said.

"I thought your PA announcements were quality and thoughtful," I assured him.

"I'm surprised you haven't gotten a sit down with Donna yet after your farting stunt in front of the Superintendent," David redirected. "When do you think you'll hear about that?"

"Soon, but possibly not just for that if my day goes according to plan."

"Well keep me posted, watching this train wreck is quite enjoyable," David said, and I left to go back to my classroom. Diane had somehow made it to her room in spite of the slog of a walk she had to do to train her new pet. I started focusing on my end of things again. I had my posters made and I was putting those up this morning. I had my stickers to put on the assignments from yesterday but those wouldn't be graded today, and I think I was only going to seriously look at one hour to find some truly terrible comments from students to mock.

I had managed to get the computer cart booked, so I had laptops that the students were using to do some tests on a computer simulation. It was perfect to keep them occupied so I could work, and I had booked a couple other upcoming dates to keep lesson planning simple. The students were happy since they got to work in pairs and got a computer. All of a sudden I heard a commotion coming from Diane's room. I stepped outside and went through the main door to see what was going on. She had taken a physics ramp that is like a air hockey table. Then she had managed to construct a container that allowed her to hold the turtle on the sliding portion of the ramp. The students were analyzing data of the acceleration of the turtle at different angles. Or most of the students were. There were a couple students who were clearly not happy about the assignment and refused to participate.

Diane noticed that I had come in. "It will be helpful for blind physicists," she explained.

"A growing population in Michigan," I nodded along. A student giggled nearby us. One of the students that was refusing to torture the turtle rolled her eyes. "I'm glad that the rocket projectile unit isn't until later for the sake of the turtle," I added. Diane's eyes lit up at my comment. I wasn't sure if I regretted giving her a potential idea because I was curious to see if she could actually launch rockets with something attached and I trusted her to do something hilarious yet not actually torturing of animals. Although, on the other hand, the turtle ramp was pretty far over the line. I hoped the turtle wouldn't poop on the ramp and clog the air holes. I started leaving to head back to my classroom but on the way, I told a group of students, "If you take a picture of that turtle on the ramp, it will be a shellfie." They laughed but it was mostly out of pity, I think.

When I got back to my room every student was working diligently. I was a little bit surprised, but I suppose the last few days had been very odd for them, so it made a little bit of sense that they weren't acting up. I took attendance and checked my email. Donna had sent me an email asking if we could meet at lunch or on my prep period to talk about yesterday. I was pretty sure that I would rather meet on my prep so I could still plan with everyone at lunch but I wanted to check first before responding. I left my room again and headed over to Josh first. He was lecturing the class, but when I walked in he told them they could work on whatever for a couple of minutes.

"Donna wants to meet with me today either at lunch or on my prep," I told him. "I assume prep is better for us."

"I think so, what are you going to say when she asks you to explain?" Josh asked me. I hadn't thought about how I would interact with her. I always assumed I would do something stupid and then be fired, but I hadn't thought over the logistics of being fired.

"I don't know," I said finally. "I guess I shouldn't apologize too much or she'll never fire me, but I don't really want to be rude either. Maybe I'll just keep brushing her off while acting normal."

"Don't get fired today though, at least wait until we put out your first video or something good," Josh continued. "Diane's turtle thing today was hilarious."

"Did you know she's using the turtle for her physics lesson?" I asked. Josh laughed and shook his head no. "A couple of students looked mighty pissed off."

"I bet they were," Josh replied and smiled. "Go check with Emily and Christine, but I say meet on prep and we can plan it a bit at lunch." I left and went to see Emily next. She was just sitting on her computer while her students drew maps of places and labelled them in Spanish. She agreed we should discuss this at lunch first. I briefly let Christine know the plan and then headed back to email Donna. The bell rang on my way back and the first hour students had cleaned up nicely. As second hour trickled in, I emailed Donna to let her know I was busy at lunch but would stop by her office on my prep hour. I got a response from her quickly that said she would come by my room. That probably meant I wasn't going to be fired, but I also wondered if I should take down my student ranking poster. No student had noticed it yet or at least if they had nobody said anything about it.

The next two hours went by and I planned some script stuff for after school and thought about some explanations that were reasonable, but not too reasonable, for what happened yesterday. At lunch I ran over my thoughts with the crew and they offered some alternatives, but none that seemed better to me. We went through my emails and I found one to respond to.

Dear Mr. Miles,

I am John's mother and I was talking to him about getting some extra help. He told me that you said you are unavailable most days at lunch. When would be a good time for him to get help?
Thanks!
Mrs. Maxworthy

I quickly typed out a response and hit send.

Class?

I think that one word replies are frequently sufficient and this was definitely one of those cases. I never understood why teachers put so much effort into providing alternate times for learning that weren't during class. That's what the class time is for. If that's not working, adjust what the student is doing during class.

Then it was prep and I waited for Donna to show up. Within two minutes she was there and came in without knocking. She looked serious and also exasperated.

"Hi Donna, how are you doing?" I asked.

"I'm a bit worn out, it's busy but I'm hoping to catch a break this weekend and relax now that the school year is up and running."

"Hey, I'm sorry about yesterday when the Superintendent was here," I started to explain. "Obviously the lesson timing wasn't great for an unannounced visit, and I was a little tired from planning a vacation that my wife and I are going to go on soon."

"Look Scott, I'm a big fan of your work. I know you do a lot of great teaching with the students and everything. Just don't let it happen again and make sure the next time the superintendent is around you don't make me look like a complete fool." I felt bad for putting her in a bad spot, but not bad enough to not go after the bonus winnings.

"I'll try, but you know how it is," I responded. My goal was to apologize a little but also bring up a trip that I wasn't actually planning so that she wouldn't think I had a good reason for diving under the desk. Then I wanted to pretend like nothing was a big deal at all so she would leave annoyed.

"I'm not really sure what you mean," Donna responded with a look on her face that was part annoyed and part confused. "Just make sure you make up for that one because it was really out of character, and I'm not pleased about what happened." I could feel her regaining her irritation but also getting ready to leave. I think I played it well. Donna got up to leave, and I turned back to the computer. She shook her head and walked over to Diane's classroom. I heard a commotion and peaked through the window. Donna was not thrilled about the turtle sliding down the ramp even though this hour had no protestors.

Donna started screaming. "Why do you keep pulling stunts like this? In the twenty years you've been teaching here you've never done anything wrong and this is now the third example in the last week?" The two moved to the hallway.

"Diane responded angrily, "You may not speak to me that way about how I teach my lessons and especially not in front of my classroom filled with students!"

I jumped in without thinking. "That was really inappropriate Donna." Diane and Donna both looked at me, Diane's face started to smile or laugh but quickly changed back to a serious one before Donna turned.

Donna was flustered and angry. "I will take a minute to calm down but we will be meeting again and soon. That turtle needs to be gone by the end of the day and may not return." She stormed off.

"Uh oh," I said after she had turned the corner. "Looks like we're both in trouble." I emphasized trouble in a long slow mocking tone. Diane smiled and walked back into her classroom. I checked in on the class, and I had some new emails. I starred them so we could work out some responses tomorrow.

Chapter 7 Chemistry with White Jesus

After school I went to Emily's room to get my makeup and costume ready. She had taken the costume from Josh and added a wig. I got dressed in her side store room for her class. It felt really weird and pretty inappropriate. If I didn't have three other people counting on me, I would have backed out. Emily put some various makeup things that I was unfamiliar with on my face and my eyes. I had on a white robe, a wig and she had even shaded in my face to make it look like I had facial hair. I snuck back to my classroom to shoot the video. I put up the problems we would go through on the interactive whiteboard and set up my floating football helmet. I hit record and started. I held out my arms wide and said, "When I went ashore, I saw a large crowd of subscribers and I felt compassion for them for that we were like sheep without a shepherd; and I began to teach them chemistry. Welcome to chemistry with Jesus."

I gave an introduction to what specific heat capacity is, what units it has, and an example of how the specific heat capacity of water differs from metals. Then I started on problem one.

"And the angel of the Lord appeared to him in a flame of fire out of the midst of a bush. He looked and behold; the bush was burning but was not consumed. If the fire was used to heat 147 g of water from room temperature (26 °C) to a blazing temperature of 87 °C, how much heat was used? Exodus 3 Verse 2 Chapter 3 Page 111. I worked out the solution on the whiteboard and then ended by saying, "Let's thank God for significant figures which allow us to represent our answer with truth and respect towards our measuring apparatus." Then I wrote 37,000 J on the board and circled it.

I completed another problem about where two disciples argued over what the answer to the question would be. Next I lowered my head. "Now let us pray. Dear God, please let us do well on our chemistry tests. Even marginal would suffice. Only a miracle is going to save this hot mess. Amen." Then I wrapped up by saying, "And he began teaching on his YouTube channel and was liked and subscribed by all. Don't forget to subscribe, like this video and leave a comment. If you send this video to ten friends good things will come to you, think about What Would Chemistry Jesus Do?" and I wrote #WWCJD on the whiteboard before turning towards the camera, smiling, then bowing my head.

The video was bold, funny and was completely out of line. It was perfect. I quickly went home and started editing. I added in some flames to the first problem solution and then an angel put them out with water that had 4.18 embedded on the extinguisher. I added some fireworks at the end and some daring music at the start. I set the editing software to create the final file and went to go cook dinner. I looked around and decided it was going to be a pizza night rather than something that wasn't appetizing. I ordered some deep dish and some pizza that had the cheese stuffed into the crust. They were both amazing, and I wasn't in the mood to choose. I was celebrating. After eating, I uploaded the file to the internet and filled in all of the search terms. I put together a close-up image with big giant letters of WWCJD over the picture of me writing out the solution. The title I put Learning Chemistry with White Jesus - Episode 1 Specific Heat Capacity. Then I tweeted out the link. Tomorrow I would assign the video to all of my chemistry classes.

On Wednesday students turned in another simulation experiment they completed in class on the computers from the computer cart. I put the homework assignment on the board with instructions on how to access the video but not what the video was about. At lunch we had a lot of work to get done. The video was now out, we had to prepare for the staff meeting, and I was on the lookout for Donna. She hadn't contacted me, and Diane said that she hadn't heard from her since the yelling yesterday. I also had emails that we could get to if we had time. The four of us met in my classroom for lunch.

"The video was funny," Josh remarked.

"Easy for you to say, you're not the one that's going to get struck by lightning," I argued.

"What are the odds that you get hit by lightning and win the lottery?" Emily asked.

Josh counted on his fingers for an excessive amount of time. "Seven."

"We need to make plans for the staff meeting today, talk about my next meeting with Donna, and I also have an email to respond to finally."

Dear Mr. Miles,
We were wondering what we could do to help Peter
improve his grade in your class. He's doing well in all
of the other classes but can't seem to figure chemistry
out.
Sincerely,
Mr. and Mrs. Peters

"Wait so his name is Peter Peters?" Christine observed.

"Yep," I noted. "It was an odd choice. This kid has turned in absolute garbage work all year, never tries hard in class and also he's doing poorly in three other classes."

"I think I can pull this email off," Christine started typing up a draft.

Dear Mr. and Mrs. Peters,
Peter hasn't been indicating a desire to
improve his grade. His assignments show little effort
and thinking and his classroom participation would
also show a comfort level with his current grade. I
also see multiple grades in the gradebook that are
lower than his chemistry grade and am unclear on
why you lied about this to me.
Sincerely,
Mr. Miles

"I was going to use the f-word more, but I suppose this works," I commented. Then I clicked send. "So does anyone know what we're doing at the staff meeting today?"

"Definitely something that will forever change the face of our teaching," Josh snarked.

"I think you should tell everyone to shut up at the beginning of the meeting, how hard is it to be an adult and listen respectfully for once?" Christine added.

"I would like to apologize for offending you by talking occasionally," I said in the sincerest tone possible. Christine laughed.

"I disagree," Emily thought out loud. "If you're going to do something at the beginning, everyone will forget by the middle and end of the meeting because it's probably going to be something stupid that we meet about. I say start a chant in the middle of the meeting about whatever BS they're selling and we'll all help pick it up."

"That's true," agreed Josh. "Diane might try something too, so if you run out of ammo first no one will remember it."

"Give us a raise, give us a raise," I started chanting.

"Woah, woah, let's not get all communist here," Emily snarked.

"I agree with Emily that all chants should encourage communism," Josh said in a surprisingly serious tone. It caught us off guard and we all paused awkwardly before a small amount of giggling ensued.

"What if the meeting is encouraging communist teaching in the classroom?" I challenged the group.

"Again?" Josh asked. I nodded and he sighed. "Whatever it is, I say you and I sit together and come up with a plan to challenge whatever it is they bring. I think the odds are in our favor that it will be something absurd based on statistics of our previous staff meetings."

"Then Christine and I can sit on the opposite side of the room to spread whatever you start," Emily added. "Just don't get too fancy with all the big French words like statistics."

"You speak French," Josh rebutted.

"Sí," Emily agreed.

"Ooh, I got a response from Mrs. Peters," I announced. This time it is just from her and I pulled the email up on the projector.

Dear Mr. Miles,
I do not find it appropriate for you to be doing background checks on students that are working hard to improve themselves. As a fellow educator I work hard to capitalize on any student trying to succeed at any moment and I question your decision to pass up an opportunity. This is very disappointing and perhaps I will need to follow up with your supervisor.
Mrs. Peters

"She pulled out the fellow educator line," I announced.

"It must be hard for her to be right all of the time," Emily snarked. "What a lousy parent."

"Hey, if covering up your children's laziness so that they can get into a college that they don't actually deserve is lousy parenting, well, I," Josh got stuck.

"Yep, that would be the end of the thought I think," I helped. I started typing my response and decided to mix things up a bit. "What do you think of this?" I surveyed the group.

Haha, nope!

"No salutation?" Emily asked incredulously. "That is bold and I like it." Good enough for me I thought. I clicked send and then directed the rest of her responses to go immediately to my trash folder. There was a knock on my door and Donna came in. She looked surprised to see our meeting and shook it off and told me that she needed to see me in her office during my prep hour later. Then she went over to Diane's room. We heard a knock and assumed she was saying the same thing.

"I hope she's not firing you today," Christine lamented. "I haven't even gotten the t-shirt I ordered to arrive yet."

"I doubt she'll skip straight to firing," Josh assured us. "Although if so, I guess we'll just have to go get our millions of dollars and wipe up our tears with big piles of cash." I agreed with Christine in my head. This had been a lot of fun and we were setting up all of these funny things to do and who knows what Diane's team was coming up with. I wasn't ready to transition into my new life yet and I hoped this was just a reprimand. We talked briefly about how to handle the meeting and then the bell rang. Emily left first and then Christine and finally Josh right before the late bell sounded. None of us were ever in a hurry like we used to be and surprisingly nothing bad seemed to come of it. It was very freeing to just be able to not rush through the day, and I liked the impact on our mental health. We all smiled and laughed more. And even though we occasionally were dropping mind games on our students, they seemed to be better off as well.

By the time my prep came up, I had gotten slightly nervous. I wondered if I should apologize better to try and prolong things. But I also didn't want to prolong them so that Diane could get fired immediately after my meeting. Finding that balance was making me stressed. I went down right away even though I figured it was less strategic. I had to know what was going to happen. Maurice saw me come in and told me to wait for a second. I sat down in one of his chairs and he went into Donna's office. Then he came back out.

"I'm really sorry Scott, but she has to handle an emergency that came up," Maurice apologized. "She might be busy for a while, so I will call if she finishes, but probably she'll talk to you tomorrow instead." He sounded serious enough that it felt like I was going to be in trouble. But I figured if it was just her in there, then she wasn't planning on firing anyone or she would have a human resources person with her. Unless that person had left when the emergency came up. I stopped by Josh's room and talked to him about what had happened. Then I stopped by to check in with Diane. David and Darnell were in her room chatting with her while her students worked on a worksheet.

"Must be nice to be able to just pass out a worksheet and all of your students work the whole hour," I observed.

Diane stretched her arms lazily. "Yes, it sure is nice indeed." She smiled and asked me, "So did you get to Donna before the emergency happened?"

"Nope, looks like we'll get fired tomorrow," I responded.

"I don't think anyone's getting fired tomorrow," David argued. David was wearing a t-shirt with a giant smiley face emoji on it. I noticed that Diane had constructed a big photo frame that said in big letters "Students that are annoying me currently." In the frame was a photo of a student I recognized from her second hour.

"Are we all eating lunch together tomorrow still or are we waiting until the weekend to hang out and socialize?" Darnell asked.

"Let's do both," I said. This has been fun, but it'd be better if we got to check in with each other a couple of times a week. So far it had been just the four of us somewhat isolated. Did you guys send any emails this week?"

"It's the best being able to write anything you want," Darnell said and smiled. "I actually look forward to emails at this point. I wonder if I can pull a parent in to conference."

"I have one," David paused and grinned. "I've been telling them that I was too busy to respond but I would get back to them tomorrow. Then I keep sending that message every day. It's been going for four days now." Darnell laughed like he was involved in constructing the emails a little bit.

Darnell added, "I've been grading their work still, but when I grade it I just put confusing comments on the papers without reading anything and pass them back. Whenever they ask about what I meant I tell them I'm not here to spoon feed them the information and that if they're actually trying they'd know what to do."

Diane had been impatiently waiting to tell another story. "So Mary caught a student cheating earlier in the year and the kid denied it and the parents threw a tantrum so he wouldn't get punished, and it worked. So she gave him really hard alternate exams and then when the parents emailed her she wrote her email to include the word lie in as many words as possible. She italicized "lie" every time too. It was beautiful, or I guess I should say beLIEvable and resiLIEnt."

I wanted to share some of our glory as well. "I just sent an email to parent that pulled the "as a fellow educator" card out. I wrote 'Haha, nope' and nothing else. If we make it another week, they're going to have to make statues of us for properly responding to parents. So how come no turtle today or are we expecting a unicorn tomorrow?"

Diane laughed. "There will be an animal tomorrow, it took some strings to pull off. You won't want to be absent."

"I'll look forward to it at lunch," I said jovially. "Unless it is part of our lunch in which case, I will reserve judgement until I find out what the animal is." I headed out to let them do any more planning. It was nice to catch up a little bit. We had been pretty separate so far this week and I looked forward to sharing stories tomorrow and over the weekend.

Chapter 8 A Below Average Staff Meeting

After school I headed to our staff meeting right away. No one ever got to staff meetings early, and this one was being run by Eric. When I got there, it was just him setting up a PowerPoint on the big screen. I wondered if I could get a sneak preview to start planning. I had brought a notebook and pens to make plans during the meeting. Our meetings were in a really nice room that was never available to teachers because it was used by administrators and clubs all of the time. It had high quality everything with a couple glaring exceptions. The sound system never worked well. Either the microphone wasn't charged or there was obnoxious feedback and the presenter would have to yell. Sometimes the microphone just wouldn't connect to the sound system and so we had a lot of frustrating meetings getting yelled at but still unable to hear. It would hurt your brain to try and focus in such an odd setting. But the furniture was nice and the room was so spacious that it made a lot of us a bit jealous that we couldn't get things like this in our classrooms. Maybe after all of our donations the remaining staff would.

"Hey Eric," I said casually after setting my stuff down in a good location. "Are you running the show this afternoon?"

"Yep, hopefully everything works," he replied without getting distracted from his set up.

"Better check the microphone now or you'll have a five-minute delay making it operational," I suggested. Eric laughed dismissively. Soon a few staff members starting walking in, and Josh was one of the early ones. I told him to see if he could figure anything out from Eric. The cover slide of the PowerPoint that was up on the screen just said "Welcome Staff" and had the date and time of the meeting.

Josh walked up and started asking some questions to Eric and then came back a couple minutes later. "He said he'll tell us all in a few minutes, but that he has to set some things up still and didn't want to spoil the surprise," Josh informed me. I saw Christine and Emily walk in together. They waved and sat in the middle of the other side of the room. Diane and Mary walked in together and came over to say hello. Mary had on a sweater with a garden hoe on it that said "GMOs before Hoes." Diane asked if I had gotten everything situated for practice. I told her the captains were running practice and that tomorrow I'd take them out on a run but she'd get Friday. They sat at a table nearby us and Darnell and David joined them a minute later. By the time the meeting was supposed to start, a line of teachers formed as most people arrived one to two minutes before the start and we all were supposed to sign in. God forbid we were trusted to show up to staff meetings, but instead we had our typical three-minute delay until an administrator finally got frustrated and asked everyone to sign in later. The crowd noise grew quite loud as teachers reveled in the opportunity to speak to other adults. There was a healthy mix of venting and non-school related discussion going on when Eric started the meeting.

The start of the meeting was a sixty second process where Eric asked everyone to sit down and be quiet, then he shouted the same instructions, then he had a side conversation, then started his presentation, then stopped to try again to get people to sit down and several steps then repeated. David finally yelled, "It's not that hard to shut up so we can start the meeting. Be an adult and pay attention." It was beautiful although Eric looked shocked and uncomfortable with the aggression for a moment.

Eric started his presentation. "So some of the central office administration has been looking over some data from our goals. They have concerns with the number of students struggling to learn and not improving. What they've decided to focus on is below average students." He flipped to a new slide showing some bar graphs. "We're going to spend some time revising our goals and the focal point of your goals must be on reducing the number of below average students. We'd like to move all of the below average to either average or above average, and we're hoping the average student group will move up along the way."

Josh's hand shot up. Eric saw the hand and was trying to decide whether to ignore it and keep presenting. Josh removed the opportunity and just started speaking loudly to the group. "Did I hear that correctly that the administration wants us to have all students score above average on our tests that we're administering?"

"Yes," Eric replied. He started to change the slide but Josh interrupted again.

"So you're telling me, that in a meeting of college graduates who have dedicated their lives to learning, that none of them was competent to understand that it's not mathematically possible for all students to score above average? That even if the lower end groups move up in scores, they will just push the bar for average up as well leaving us with a higher achieving set of below average students." The crowd started to make noise. At first it was some teachers explaining to others why this made no sense and then it was teachers reacting to the stupidity coupled with the idea of having to redo our goals that were such a pain in the first place.

I seized the moment. "What if we don't change our goals?" I shouted. "We had to spend a lot of time, we don't get anything out of them, and this is a spit in the face to us. We're being given a mathematically impossible goal and we're just supposed to pretend it isn't some stupid individual that spent two years in the classroom before getting an undeserved pay raise for less important work than what we do." The room had quieted down as I was being very aggressive with my language.

Then Diane stepped in. She stepped onto her table and started chanting. "NO MORE GOALS! NO MORE GOALS!"

Emily and Christine joined in and Josh, David, Darnell, Mary and I also started shouting, "NO MORE GOALS! NO MORE GOALS!" The rest of the crowd was somewhat puzzled but also clearly upset and the noise started to grow. Eric had been thrown initially but now was realizing he needed to quell the uprising quickly.

"That's enough!" he shouted. "This is not the means to have this discussion, and I won't have this at my meeting." The noise ceased suddenly.

I took another swing. "My new goal is going to be for the central office administration to not have below average ideas!" Laughter erupted and even Eric had to turn his face for a second to hide his smile.

Diane stepped up again. "Anyone that supports this is working against students and against a climate that values intelligence. If the curriculum person that came up with this doesn't apologize to our staff, we're not doing anything!"

Eric wanted to gain control but because Diane and I were both serving up comments he didn't know how to take both of us out of the room at once. Finally he stated, "I understand your concerns but this is not the time nor the methodology for addressing them. After my presentation I will speak to both of you to make sure that I have your concerns and I will share them with the appropriate people." He was good! We both sat back and relaxed for a bit to wait for another opportunity to proclaim the stupidity of these ideas. Diane shot me a wink and a gun, and I laughed.

Eric continued with a timeline. "We'll start by reviewing which of our current goals are designed for all students instead of focusing on the below average students."

Josh shouted again, "I'm sorry, but I just have to make sure that I understand this one more time. This was an actual conclusion made by adults? They expect all students to achieve at an above average level relative to each other?"

Eric mostly ignored him. "That was addressed earlier. Continuing on we will be looking for methods to increase our impact on below average students. In particular the district was concerned that nearly half of our students scored below average."

Josh stood up and then restrained himself from speaking. So I went for the third attack. "Look, Eric, we appreciate that you're trying to put on this presentation, but this is so unbelievably dumb that it's insulting for us as professionals to have to try and ignore how brazenly stupid it is. How are we supposed to pretend that a district not knowing that it's impossible to not have below average students when comparing relative to their peers in that district? Of course about fifty percent of students are below average. That's how math works! I mean who came up with this garbage in the first place?"

Eric hesitantly responded, "This came from a committee, not one person."

"Multiple adults together analyzed data, and this was what they concluded?" Josh asked incredulously.

"Yes." Eric understood how stupid all of this was but was doing his best to pretend it was normal. "Moving along. Our goal is to have a 20% increase in above average students by two years from now to end up with 70% above average and 30% below average. Then by 5 years we'd like to get to 100% of students above average. Obviously that's not going to happen, but hopefully we at least get 90% students above average with a few at average." The next slide showed the bars changing from 50/50 to 70/30 to 100/0 with different emojis for each one. Then the next slide had some examples of current goals and revised goals that focused on below average students.

Diane raised her hand. Eric nodded at her. "Hi, is there any concern that if we do poorly that we'll end up with all students below average?" Josh laughed and I snickered. Diane continued, "In particular, I'm concerned about Scott Miles producing so many students that are below average and making us all look bad."

"I share these concerns," I admitted.

"I'm also concerned about Scott," Darnell added. Josh was barely holding on, and he burst into laughing when Darnell spoke.

Eric tried to regain composure. "Look, we're all aware that Scott is going to ruin this for most of us, and the district was smart enough to anticipate that and put in safeguards so that Scott doesn't bring everyone down with him."

"They did not!" I shouted.

"It's true," Eric explained. "You'll see on the next slide here." Eric flipped the slide which was just some graphs of historic trends of how many students were below average. At this point most teachers were in hysterics. "Ok seriously though, historically our number of below average students has mostly maintained in spite of all of the changes that our teachers have implemented. This is why we're shifting focus on the below average students instead."

There was a loud knock on the door. Diane jumped up and announced, "I'll get it." It was a pizza delivery person. Diane paid him some cash and said, "This is one of my students from two years ago." A few teachers said hello from their seats. "Hey Charlie, how many of your customers are above average tippers?"

The pizza delivery guy laughed. "Well, I don't know for sure, but I'd guess around half of them are above average and half below average." The crowd of teachers burst into applause and a triumphant Diane returned to her table where her friends starting dividing up the pizza amongst themselves. It smelled amazing. Eric looked like he was ready to explode. Then he walked over to the computer to calm himself and flipped to the final slide. It was about meeting in our groups to analyze and revise our goals.

"I'll be meeting with the pizza group unless there's a dark chocolate group," I announced loudly enough for most, but not all, to hear. A few teachers got into their groups like they were supposed to, a few just flat out left, and the eight of us joined together to eat a couple of slices while chatting before leaving. Eric quietly dipped out. It was our best staff meeting yet.

Chapter 9 The Reprimand

I came in a bit earlier on Thursday to set up an actual lesson. I was missing doing some actual teaching, and I also realized it wouldn't be long until I wouldn't be teaching anymore. Maybe if Diane got fired first, I'd even stay for a week or two to give them some time to find a new teacher. When I got in I opened my email. I had a few from parents, but I was busy so I just marked them and figured we'd go through them at lunch. I had one from Emily that was sent to all staff and said she had also managed to get a grant from a generous donor for supplies while also mentioning the absurdity of filling out five different forms to be able to buy anything. I headed over to the room where she was to see what she had brought. We chatted for a bit about the staff meeting and periodically a teacher came in and took some supplies and thanked her. One of the teachers had some choice language about how obnoxious our policy for ordering was. No one had noticed yet that she had her grading stickers in the piles.

I left and grabbed some caffeine in the form of sugary pop goodness and headed back to finish getting ready for teaching. I was doing a demonstration where I mixed hot metal with cold water and looked at how the temperatures changed. This was one of my favorites because it seemed simple and obvious until students started explaining things. I had four different metals that were all the same mass but not the same size. I put them into a boiling water bath to let them heat up to 100 °C.

When class was ready, I immediately started showing them the boiling water bath and explaining what I was going to do. I put the zinc metal into an insulated cup and wrote the temperature changes on the board. Then I did the same thing with aluminum, tin and copper. I told the students to make a whiteboard showing the thermal and phase energy changes for one of the metals and the water it mixed with.

They split into groups, made whiteboards and then with about twenty minutes left in the hour we sat in a circle and discussed them. Students talked about the energy changes, how much, how the transfer of energy happened. I asked the students what does it mean that the metal particles changed temperature more than the water particles? How could the metal particles slow down a lot while the water particles didn't speed up very much?

The room grew quiet as students thought about it. I was going to have them turn to their neighbor to chat when a hand went up. I nodded at Arul and he started to explain, "Well whenever I'm not sure about temperature and heat, I turn to the Bible for explanations." The class started laughing and discussing the video wildly. I had forgotten about the video assignment because I had been preoccupied with thinking about the staff meeting and then setting up class. I laughed for a minute along with them.

"Are we going to see more chemistry with white Jesus?" another student asked.

"I have no idea what you're talking about," I said coyly.

"He was pretty helpful at explaining things, and I think he saved my soul from eternal damnation," Emma explained. Emma was one of my very sarcastic students with a quality sense of humor.

"That's sounds like winning all around," I commented. I wondered if any of my emails I was checking later would be related. The bell was about ready to ring, so I left things at that. We briefly summarized what we learned today and then the bell rang and first hour left. I quickly started the hot water bath to be ready by the time second hour started. I hadn't rushed to set up a lesson since we had won, and I remembered being in a hurry to get an experiment ready and how I never seemed to have time to make it to the bathroom on some of those days. Second and third hour followed a similar sequence. In third hour one of my students gave an incredibly brilliant explanation of how the metal didn't require a lot of energy from the hot water bath to heat to 100 °C and so when it cooled back down it did not give a lot of energy back. Her phrasing was elite, and I asked her to repeat what she said and then asked another student to repeat what he had heard from her.

As third hour was ending, Josh came in. He had left his class a bit early because Emily's sub had come in the cover him. "Hey, I wanted to check in with you briefly before we go eat with David, Diane, Darnell and Mary," he explained. "Do you think we could meet after school to do some email stuff and maybe set up a plan for next week?"

"I have to run practice today, but I can send you the emails I got this morning, and we can talk about it after I get home or tomorrow," I offered.

"That works, are you ok if Emily and Christine and I meet without you?" he asked.

"Yeah, that's fine. Just send me a message if there's anything I need to know or do. Let's go get some lunch though," I said as I got up to lock up and move to the lounge.

Josh and I were somehow the last two to arrive at lunch. There were other teachers present, so we talked about the meeting, but we were careful with our language and phrasing. It was nice having others present actually because it removed the contest from our conversation and it was just a normal lunch like we used to have. We were having a meat, cheese and pasta lunch. There was a lot of shredded cheese, some slices and cubes for snacks. We had lunch meats, pulled pork and some grilled chicken. Then we mixed those in with some fettuccine alfredo and I brought in cheese filled tortellini. It was an odd line up, but I was definitely a fan. I mixed all kinds of combinations on a plate and then heated it up in the microwave for a little bit.

David and Emily were talking about who would host this weekend. I suggested we chip in and rent out a room at a bar. A teacher that used to work for the school had quit a while ago. Now she ran a bar they called The Teacher's Lounge which would be perfect, and we could put our money towards a former colleague. Then Diane redirected our conversation back to the staff meeting. "Calling out the bullshit at that meeting was epic," she stated. "I haven't felt that good about a staff meeting in a while. Who are these people that get hired and yet don't understand basic mathematics well enough to run a school?"

"You have to wonder what the interview looked like for some of these," Mary pointed out.

"I'm guessing there was an overwhelming amount of educational jargon in that interview on both sides," Christine articulated.

"What is your interdisciplinary literacy mission statement and how does this lead to a decrease in below average achievement?" Diane interviewed me.

"A diverse commitment to differentiation of objectives written on the board," I replied.

"Needs more goal statement revisions," Darnell objected.

"Oh my goodness, I am not changing my goals again," I noted. "I wonder if we can get a group of teachers to all commit to not changing our goals."

"Should we start a petition?" Diane asked.

"A shared petition?" I asked.

"I think I know six signatures we could easily obtain," Diane observed.

"A group project I think we could all get behind," Josh agreed. "Let's talk about it some more on Saturday. By the way, the salami wrapped around some tortellini is amazing." We spent some time talking about meats and cheeses and then headed back to class.

I walked in a bit too late for fourth hour, so the water bath wasn't ready when the bell rang. They took advantage and started asking me a lot of questions about my homework assignment.

"Was that actually you?"

"Did you get struck by lightning?"

"Do teachers get trained on how to dress up as Jesus in college?"

"Can Jesus help me with math?"

"If I go to church, can I get extra credit?"

I told them that I had no idea of what Jesus's future plans were, but that he had enjoyed teaching them chemistry. We finally started the lesson, but by the time we were ready for discussion, we were a few minutes behind still and the discussion was rushed and not very good. I tried, but it just never really got going and when the bell rang I figured I should head over to Donna's office and see if she was ready to talk to me still.

Maurice smiled and motioned for me to sit in the chair. He went into her office and then came out quickly and said, "She's ready for you."

"Thanks," I replied and walked in quietly. I still couldn't seem to prepare myself properly for these situations. I had a weird combination of emotions. I felt bad for making Donna's work even harder, I felt confused because I had to restrain my typical apologies, and I felt a bit motivated to try and win by being strategic.

"Hi Miles, have a seat please," Donna motioned to her table. I sat down. Donna started explaining that the events that had taken place had gone out of her control and that she had done her best to protect me, but that she was required to take a disciplinary action.

"Am I fired?" I asked incredulously. I probably shouldn't have asked it so emotionally but it just came out.

"No," Donna said suddenly. "Of course not." She was quick to reassure that but her tone made it clear something was happening. "But you are in trouble. There's going to be a disciplinary letter put into your file about the behavior in front of the superintendent. In addition, I heard that you and a few others were being disruptive at the staff meeting yesterday. You need to get yourself together."

"I see," I said. I was thinking about how best to play this situation. It was good that an actual discipline process was starting and I was trying to think on how I should react that would be strategic. Donna seemed to mistake that for me being terrified.

"Look Scott, nobody is going to get fired," Donna tried to assure me. You don't need to worry about that. I can't even hire a new teacher let alone a chemistry or a physics teacher. You just need to worry about making a better impression around the important people. You also need to control yourself and not be goofy all of the time. We understand you work with teenagers, but you need to be able to switch in and out of modes."

That wasn't the speech I was really hoping for. "What happened to the math position you were trying to hire?" I asked.

"It's still open," she explained. "There were two applicants, but neither was qualified. I tried calling some employees that retired, some that left to other districts, but no one was interested. I'm stuck filling it with a substitute and myself. So again, you don't need to panic; I just need you to do better next time. There's no way anyone is getting fired here. The state of Michigan has made it where it's impossible for us to do that because there aren't any students going into teaching and too many teachers have moved out of state due to pay cuts. And I'm not just trying to say that's the only reason you're not fired. I know the good work you do and how you get students to think. But I was very embarrassed by your stunt and I'm not thrilled about the staff meltdowns going on."

This was a lot of information that I was glad to hear, but also worried about the message. I always worried when I was new that I would do something stupid and get fired from a parent complaint. But this conversation was making it sound like it was going to take a monumental effort to get fired. I needed to talk to Diane. "Ok, I need to go work on something if that's ok," I stated and got up to leave.

"Thanks Scott, I'll check in with you later," Donna replied. "If you want to file a counter letter to your letter just give it to Maurice and he'll put it in your file."

I went straight to Diane's room. She had the students doing a friction activity where they dragged different objects around the room. The objects were childlike dolls that had leashes attached to them. It was weird. Maybe a little bit funny, but definitely weird too. She was playing on her computer while the students did the experiment. "Hey I just checked in with Donna," I informed her.

She looked up from her computer, "Oh, I did too earlier today. I got a letter in my file." Diane smiled.

"I'm worried that she's not going to be able to fire us," I threw it right out there.

"She tried to reassure me of that too, but I don't believe that for a second," Diane explained. "One, from her perspective she isn't ready to fire us, but as time continues that will change. Two, it's not always her decision. The school board or human resources will often be the one to make that call, and they probably don't care whether they can hire someone to replace us or not. In fact, you pulling the stunt in front of the Superintendent was helpful to both of us."

"But what about the fact that she still hasn't found a replacement teacher for the math class? And both of us teach subjects that aren't overloaded with replacements. Especially since there hasn't been a raise for the teachers in years. I know every few years they put together a partial 0.5% raise to a few teachers to allow them to say they gave a raise, but they aren't fooling anyone and the number of teachers has plummeted."

141

"Look, I understand there aren't replacements," Diane argued. "But this district has never cared about that. They let teachers leave without a second thought as to who will replace them constantly. Don't think that you're special, I hope I beat you to it, but if I don't, they will fire you and won't care about if a replacement is lined up or not."

I felt a little better since Diane was letting me vent, but she also had complete confidence that we were still moving in the right direction. I trusted her and I also figured, if they won't fire us, we'll just keep having fun not doing a lot of work and doing funny things. This past week had been a blast and having low expectations for my workload had improved my mental health tremendously. I wasn't worried constantly about getting grading done the instant I got a new set of papers, and when parents tried to shift blame onto me, it just rolled right into the bucket of fun of replying at lunch.

I taught my final class of the day and enjoyed going for a nice long run with the cross-country team for practice. We did six miles and I felt great running. I kept up with the middle group and it was fun. I stretched afterwards and headed home.

Chapter 10 Chemistry Celebration

    I got to school at the same time as Diane did on Friday. She was walking in with a peacock on a leash that had a sign that said "Please don't pet me, I'm training to help blind people." It was a full-grown peacock! It had giant blue and green feathers and looked really cool although I was mildly terrified to get close to it. "You brought in a peacock?" I asked. "How did you even obtain one?" Mary walked by with a t-shirt that had a picture of Saturn and said "Back To Back Hula Hoop Championships." She gave Diane a high five while maintaining as much distance from the peacock as possible and then headed towards her room.

    Diane grinned triumphantly. "I know a guy who knows a guy." Then she winked and slowly walked the peacock around to her room. She used that bird all day long. Her students had set up an obstacle course that the peacock would run through while leashed and they would do various analysis of forces, acceleration, velocity and more from the data produced. Later in the day the peacock started making noise and it was absurdly loud.

    Fortunately, I had my own inappropriate science lesson that would potentially be as cool. I had brought some legit fireworks in. There was a training where you could set off your own fireworks so I had bought some smaller ones for inside and a few bigger fireworks to show outside. I had never done the shells and mortar type before, so I had a friend that was a professional show me the full training. It was awesome. We started by lighting some of the smaller fireworks. I did a small one in the classroom. I started to ask the students what they saw, but we quickly had to move into the hallway to let the lab ventilate so we didn't breathe in too many particulates. In the hallway we talked about what we saw, the light, the smoke, the flames, the sparks and why we saw different colors. Then we moved outside.

I set up the equipment in the middle of one of the practice fields that the sports teams and marching bands used. Then we moved towards the driveway parents used before and after school for pick up. I set down one of the medium fireworks that shot out projectiles but was not the same as the high-tech fireworks that exploded midair. A big plume of smoke formed as we watched as a dozen fireworks launched into the sky. Then I showed the class how to set up the electronics. We were ready for the show. I had the students back up to the sidelines of the field while I set up the first shell. Then I initiated the sequence. The first shell shot up into the sky before a bright green firework went off. It was louder than I anticipated and closer to the school than I felt comfortable with. Another quickly launched. This one was a red firework. It was huge. Then we did one more purple one before heading back in. The purple seemed to be louder than the first two combined. And all of them felt extremely loud because usually there's a bit more distance between the crowd and the pyrotechnics. The students were brimming with excitement. I reminded them to be quiet in the hallways while we were returning or they could expect some movement on the bottom ten poster.

Marc asked, "What if we're already on the bottom ten? Can we be loud then?" I felt slightly justified after he finished speaking.

When I got back to my room and the class settled in, it was near the end of the hour. We finished by talking about how different chemicals give off different types of light and how this allows us to identify things in space. It was a fun discussion and very engaging. But as the bell rang, Maurice came in. He said that Donna needed to see me right away and that he would take attendance for me for second hour. Before I left, I locked up all of my equipment in the middle store room and then went to tell Diane not to open anything. But she was in the store room locking up her peacock.

"Were you told to head to Donna's office as well?" she asked me.

"Yeah, who's watching your class?" I asked while peering at the window into her classroom.

"A sub that was on prep for someone else." We walked down to Donna's office together complimenting each other on our mutual creativity and boldness along the way. When we got there, we both felt good and were intellectually curious to see what was about to unfold. Diane knocked and opened the door at the same time.

"I need to speak with you one at a time," Donna explained.

"We need to get our classes rolling so whatever it is you can tell us together," Diane countered.

"I'm fine with it too," I said.

"Fine," Donna replied angrily. "Please have a seat." We both sat down facing Donna. "Scott, I have been contacted by a parent that you have started a Chemistry with Jesus YouTube video assignment. You may not produce a religious video and require your students to view it for an assignment. You also should not be producing a controversial religious video that mocks the identity of your students and the community. You need to take it down. Then I hear a noise this morning that scares me half to death and find out that it was you shooting off professional grade fireworks at school with students helping. Help me understand how you expect me to explain that to district officials concerned with safety."

"It was part of a lesson," I explained. "I've been trained by a professional on how to shoot fireworks, and it ties into the state standards. Yes, fireworks can be dangerous, but I exercised caution and good judgement throughout the lesson, as I always do. It was incredibly engaging and fireworks are a common tool to teach chemistry. If I drop a chunk of sodium in water there are hazards, but no one has concerns over the risks."

"There are to be no more fireworks used at school," Donna stated bluntly. "Am I clear?"

"I guess, but I don't know what you expect me to do for the rest of the day then," I responded. "That was kind of the lesson. I mean I'm trying my hardest to meet the needs of below average students here, and first hour was heavily engaged." Diane covered her face when I mentioned below average to try and stop herself from laughing and prevent Donna from seeing her laugh. It only worked partially.

"Diane," Donna turned towards her. "I specifically instructed you not to bring any more pets in."

"That's not true, you said I can't bring in any more turtles," Diane refuted. "This was a peacock and we used the animal for physics lessons today."

"You cannot bring in animals of any kind, let alone endangered species that could attack a student," Donna responded furiously.

"To be fair, that type of peacock is the least aggressive kind, and it is not endangered," I explained quietly. "A couple of farms have them in the area. Some students and I searched online to find out about it before first hour started."

"Do I look like I need a fucking science lesson right now?" Donna exclaimed with a glare that told us both to shut up.

"No," Diane said quietly. Donna took a moment to gather herself.

"I cannot believe the decisions you two have been making lately," Donna changed tone but was still clearly displeased. "Diane is it true you've been having students vote on how smart or stupid a student's test response is during class?" It was my turn to cover my face to hide and control my laughter.

That was funny, and I could envision Diane boldly asking the class to vote for stupid or smart. I wanted to know if she would identify the student and more details later.

"Of course that's not what we were doing," Diane calmly explained. "That's just what some student that probably is trying to push for a grade inflation is trying to describe so they can get out of learning and bump their grade up unethically. That's the problem: we let below average students get above average grades by bending the rules for them." I thought Diane was about to laugh again so I started coughing.

Donna started to erupt again, "Look you two, I get that teaching is hard and that you two both have a lot of credibility built up, but you can't go on making decisions like these. If something happens again, you'll end up with a second letter in your file."

I was curious to see how Diane would interpret Donna's reaction so I feigned fear. "Does that mean we would be fired?" I asked with a very concerned tone.

"No Scott, I told you last time, nobody is going to get fired here," Donna immediately changed her voice again. "A second letter is serious business though, and it could lead to a suspension that could possibly include no pay while you get put under review. But even there, you would return afterwards. We simply can't afford to lose teachers. But I need you to do better, and frankly I'm shocked that both of you continue to screw up like this after we just spoke.

I'm disappointed and annoyed." She paused for a moment. "I'm going to make a note of this, but I will keep it away from the central administration if nothing comes of it."

Diane turned the whole thing around, "Well I guess we'll both head back to class and try and figure out a way to teach our lessons in our classrooms without doing anything edgy."

We both got up and I played along a bit. "I know right, like English teachers don't have students read about all kinds of inappropriate sex scenes. But don't stand in front and lecture all hour either." I might have heard Donna's pencil break, but I'm not sure, and soon we were far enough away to break character. "Holy crap Diane, what do you think about us getting fired now? I mean I shot off fireworks in the field, legit pyrotechnics, and we're still like eight steps away."

"First, when you said below average students, I nearly lost it," Diane took a moment to appreciate that comment. "But I still say if we continue to do things we shouldn't, one of us will get fired. Look how mad she was, and she hasn't even found out about some of the stuff we've done yet. Have you been emailing parents back with more honesty than normal?"

I grinned and nodded. "Of course."

"Well so have we, and eventually the chaos of this will reach the school board or someone else along the way and we'll be done. What's important is that we keep having fun doing it and write a really nice apology to Donna when it becomes time. But what can we do about it at this point, we have a contract and a large amount of money on the line? Plus, this is the best thing ever. How many teachers dream of the freedom to say whatever they want to an obnoxious parent email, or some whiny student that is trying to subvert the system while others work hard?"

"We're basically heroes," I agreed. Diane flexed and I laughed. We got back to our rooms. I told Maurice that I would take it from here and he left. The students asked who he was and wanted to know if he could be our sub again in the future. I took a mental note to send him an email letting him know that later. Then I announced, "I just got back from the principal's office and she has decided not to allow our awesome chemistry lesson to happen today. We were going to do some lessons on how fireworks work and look at some high-tech samples outside, but instead you will be doing bookwork." The class was clearly disappointed and to be honest so was I. I couldn't even do anything because our contract stipulated that we were not allowed to get fired for insubordination. We had a list of what we couldn't do so that one of us didn't just violate federal law or try and sell some drugs. We wanted the process to be hilarious and creative, so we had thorough ground rules to guide everything.

I also had not had the class do bookwork since my first or second year of teaching. I told the students to do the even numbered problems at the end of chapter six but there were frequent issues with problems that were off topic from what we had learned. And each time I instructed students that they could figure out a solution themselves or I would have a spot for them on my poster.

By the time we got to lunch I was immensely bored. I had tried thinking of some new ideas to pull off next week. Fireworks had gone well but I wish that I could have done a bit more of them. I don't think any students even recorded video on their phones to share on social media. I was going to probably eventually try them in the hallway as well. Maybe I could set them off after school. Josh, Emily and Christine arrived and we ate for a bit. I filled them in on what had happened this morning.

"Sounds like progress," Christine observed.

"Or it could be a tiny amount of progress in an unreasonably long operation," I replied. I told them about the end of the meeting and how both times Donna had been very reassuring about nobody being fired.

"I think Diane is right and that someone will be fired, but we might need to up the level a bit to get there faster," Josh articulated.

"I need to write a counter letter to put into my file to refute the first one this weekend," I commented.

"I wonder if you could plagiarize a famous speech and print out an absurd number of pages that are completely disconnected," Emily proposed.

"Should I make another Chemistry with Jesus video or should I do something else instead?" I asked. I had been thinking about how I escaped the meeting with this intact, kind of, but if there was a better idea, I wasn't against changing things up.

"I think that would violate the rules since you've been specifically told not to make one. But you should make a video that talks about how great you are at chemistry but offers no teaching value at all," Josh recommended. "It would capture your true persona and also irritate the students."

"That's true," Emily agreed quickly. "I've been teaching the students Spanish incorrectly and it really annoys them when they do poorly on their tests. Mea culpa."

"What about a video for chemistry where the entire script is in Spanish?" I offered up. I thought of it as Emily was speaking, but it seemed like that could cover everything and I could offer some lame explanation of being interdisciplinary to parents and students that complained. Plus, my broken Spanish would be hilarious.

"Hola, me llamo señor," Josh started scripting.

"Me gusto muchos views-o," Christine said.

"That is a gross-o underestimation of my Spanish speaking abilities," I countered.

"Oh, speaking of Spanish, I sent a new email today," Emily shifted the conversation. "A parent had sent in this complaint about his daughter that refuses to speak in class and how their grade shouldn't be impacted by her being scared to speak. So I sent back the response that said 'solamente en español por favor.' I haven't heard back from them yet."

"Nice, hey what about professional development next week?" Josh asked.

"We have PD next week? Is it a speaker?" I asked. Ideas were forming in my head as I spoke. Some speakers were tolerable, but a few were incredibly insulting to teachers.

"Tuesday is no school for students, and we have a speaker for the first two hours of the day," Emily said as she checked her schedule. "Normally, that'd be brutal, but I bet we could get all kinds of fun revenge for speakers past."

"I say we co-plan that one with Diane's team tomorrow," I suggested.

"I completely agree," Christine replied. "With eight of us we can do more damage and this wouldn't harm any students or people we care about."

"So I'm going to make a new video today after school where I'll work out a script of bad but confident spanglish. Then tomorrow I'll work out a response letter before we meet as a group, and then at our meeting we'll make plans for Tuesday's professional development," I summarized. "Diane is running practice today so I can do the video right after school."

"Sounds bueno," Josh agreed.

"Sí," Emily nodded.

Everyone stayed and finished eating and we chatted a bit more about the funny comments that had been happening in our classrooms now that we had zero motivation to remain professional.

"So yesterday I was walking in the hallway during my prep and this kid was supposed to be going to the bathroom," Emily recounted. "Instead he was slowly stumbling down the hall on their phone. I snuck up behind him and then shouted BOO! He fell over, I was dying. He was from Mrs. Roberts class, and she makes them take a bucket to the bathroom as a pass. The bucket clanged against the floor!"

"We should start filming ourselves trying to scare students in the hallways on their phones," Christine suggested.

"Sounds like a hit new YouTube video!" I proclaimed.

"What are you going to do with your YouTube channel now that you don't need that steady stream of income?" Josh asked sarcastically.

"Apparently cyberbully teenagers," I said while shrugging my shoulders. "Which really is all I ever intended to do in the first place."

Eventually lunch ended. During the next class I told them what had happened and offered to light up a firework at the end of the hour if everyone would get their work done. They worked ambitiously all hour, and I honestly didn't care what they accomplished as long as they let me work out a script. So with six minutes left, I took one of the medium fireworks and set it outside of the classroom by leaving through the open window. It was away from the office so I figured no one would hear it and by the time word spread I could deny and pretend it was the same from this morning. I lit the wick and ran back to the window and hopped into the classroom. I'm sure other classes were interrupted because it was loud and classes on the second floor probably saw the tiny flares shooting past their rooms. I told the class not to send out any video.

During my prep I continued the script. I wanted it to be in Spanish, but the Spanish to be mildly incorrect but also incredibly confident. I needed a lesson that I knew some words about and decided to talk about temperature. I wrote some potential opening and closing lines first. Then I worked on the body along with the phrasing that I could use. I felt pretty good in the end. I had some lines that were completely correct and others where I had clearly just added a Spanish sounding ending to the end of the American words.

Sixth hour was the worst. It was the end of the day Friday and the hour dragged. But eventually the bell rang after the students had packed up and lined up way too early. I waited until the room had cleared and then I set up my recording equipment. I did one run through with the script for practice and then had a go without it.

"Hola mis estudiantes. Bienvenidos a mi clase de química," I announced to the camera. "Hoy vamos a aprender mucho de la temperatura y siempre en Español." I started drawing two squares on the board. "Este caja es caja A y esta es caja B. Caja A es metallo pero Caja B es hielo o agua. Cuando los cajos tocaran conjuntos, qué vamos a hacer? Un cajo con la temperatura diferente!" I drew the two boxes

155

coming together and changing temperature. I wrote 50 above the original box A and 10 above box B but then when I drew them together, I wrote veinte. "Es muy interesante no? Vamos a esperar por tu escribiste unas notas." I waited for a second to prolong the video a bit. "Qué es la temperatura? Es una pregunta? Tu tienes preguntas? Yo soy la respuesta por la química." Then I worked out the specific heat capacities while using the word "numeros" many times. "Gracias para tu tiempo y tus sonrisas. Hablar en el commentos por al fin!" It had devolved in the middle and it was perfect. There was almost no learning and I looked like a moron, but one that was completely confident. I took it home to start editing and also to start writing my response letter. But the family wanted to head out to eat, so I shelved everything until Saturday morning.

Rough Translation {Hello my students. Welcome to my chemistry class. Today we are going to learn a lot about temperature and always in Spanish. This box is box A and this is box B. Box A is metallic, but box B is ice or water. When the boxes touch together, what are we going to make? A box with the temperature different!
It is very interesting is it not? We are going to wait for you to wrote some notes. What is temperature? Is it a question? Do you have questions? I am the answer for the chemistry.
Thank you for your time and your smiles. To talk in the comments is the end.}

    I woke up early on Saturday and felt refreshed. It had been a busy week, but filled mostly with things that I wanted to do. I even had a comment on my video that I had spelled caja incorrectly. And I had enjoyed the week immensely and was excited to start planning next week. The eight of us were meeting at The Teacher's Lounge at 6 pm for dinner and drinks. I edited out the start and end of the video but other than that it was pretty much ready to go. I uploaded it and titled it as Chemistry Hola.

Then I started searching for famous speeches online to model my response letter after. I looked over some historical speeches and some from my favorite movies. Finally, I decided to put quotes from my favorite books without any context to match them together. I started writing.

The atrocities lobbied against myself and my team will not go unchallenged this day. Chemistry has long been thought to be second fiddle to physics, but why are all famous chemists also characterized as famous physicists? It reminds me of the scene from my chemistry text.

I then copied a full page of chemistry textbook that talked about thermodynamics. Instead of integral symbols though I just put exclamation points. I continued writing more after.

I do not believe that anyone could speak clearer than that passage on the rights of humans. But I shall continue to seek justice in all songs that speak of sunrise. My students do not seek chemistry, but it seeks for them. It is as if they sense the decline best represented by tv closed captioning for people with accents.

Then I searched for funny closed captioning errors and typed in about another page of them. I also added a preview for the high school football team that was in the local newspaper.

Finally, an appreciation of the arts will never go out of style. Not only is style to be remembered, it is to be celebrated.

And I finished out the letter by drawing shapes and signing:

Sincerely,

Scott Miles + others

The response letter was about sixteen pages long now and it was complete gibberish. I left it for everyone else to approve of and went out for a quick jog. I had no grading this weekend, which was phenomenal, although if I wanted to, I could start using our new grading stickers. After jogging I took the kids out to play at a park for a bit and then started getting ready to head out.

Chapter 11 Interdisciplinary Planning

We had a room rented at The Teacher's Lounge and their craft beer was called The Rough Draft. I preferred a lighter drink but I indulged in one out of appreciation of the clever naming. I also ordered a brownie sundae for dinner. After all, it was a celebration.

We had all arrived early and all of us were eager to share ideas as well as funny things we had done this week. Emily told her story about scaring the kid with the bucket to Darnell, David and Mary. Mary followed that up with a story about her AP biology class. "This student is concerned that she got a B+ on one test. She has a solid A in the class, but the B+ on the exam is bringing her down and it annoyed me. So I told her to get out her cell phone. She takes it out. Then I told her she couldn't leave class until she could find someone who is currently working that still cares about what grades they got in high school."

"It's crazy how much kids get hung up on grades when they matter so little later in life," Josh agreed.

Darnell switched to his AP literature class. "In AP lit I had a trivia contest and if you got a question correct you got a pack of smarties candy, but if you were wrong you got a dum dum. But the kids were totally into it and loved it so it just ended up being fun with no controversy."

"Ok, so I stole this from Miles kind of," David explained. "But I hid a bunch of potato chips under my desk. Then throughout class I would pretend to trip and fall, then crawl under the desk and then snack. Everyone in class could hear me eating chips so they knew what I was doing and I made everything obvious and then denied it each time."

Diane switched to emails. "Have you been emailing parents back? I got one doozy from a parent that was trying to get their kid that cheated on homework to not get any punishment. I sent them an email saying that this would probably work a lot better if they would send their child back to school in a cape for a few days. He did it! He wore a straight up cape to school."

"I saw that kid!" I said laughing. "Next time make him wear boots, a helmet and a cape."

Emily added, "I got a response from the parent that I wrote back saying they should only write me emails in Spanish. They wrote back a response in Spanish so I responded with "slow down, mas despacio por favor." So they revised their email in fewer words.

"You should write back in Spanish but have significant errors in it so they think you're stupid," I recommended.

"I wonder if I can pull off the please write all emails in Spanish for my math classes," Josh pondered.

"Only one way to find out," David suggested.

"Am I the only one worried that Donna is never going to fire any of us?" I asked the group.

"Not really," David replied quickly. "Last week was the most fun I've had in my career. I'm hardly grading anything and I'm doing all of the things I want to in class. All of the stressful components of teaching have melted away and it's blissful. I could do this for quite a while."

"Agreed," said Darnell. "Being able to say whatever I want and do whatever I want has been glorious. Every day I wake up with a funny thing to try, and then I just do it."

"Plus, I have to think at some point Donna will turn. I know she's insistent nobody will get fired for now, but that'll change when this keeps up," Mary stated.

"Have you guys planned anything for the professional development speaker on Tuesday?" Josh asked the others.

"We were thinking of co-planning it with you," Emily added.

Mary responded, "We planned on sitting down and working out some ideas tonight and tomorrow, but I like the idea of an eight-person team to really give the speaker hell."

"It's on differentiation and educational buzzword nonsense," David announced. "I think this is a time to stick up for all of the teachers that have to sit through this garbage."

"Differentiation?" I asked disgustedly. "They're still trying to push this idea? After all of the cognitive science research we're sitting here in the 1990s of education?"

"Not only that, but we're paying out of the nose to linger in outdated methods," Diane remarked.

"While our district can't afford to pay for steps or subs or decent pay for staff, this person gets the royal treatment I'm sure."

"Let's put in a FOIA request to find out how much they got paid!" I declared.

"And then interrupt the speaker with questions about how much they get paid the day of?" Josh asked with uncertainty.

"Yes," Mary responded. "Let's plan on splitting up and just undermining the entire presentation. Between the eight of us we can spread out and just eviscerate the whole thing." Mary was probably the kindest individual in our group. But she could dish it out when she felt it was warranted and you could sense her ire of years of sitting through boring and useless meetings and presentations. They were sometimes better now too, so she had been through some incredibly useless and insulting sessions in the past when she was new.

On Monday we got two subs for the eight of us to be able to move in and out and prepare for the next day's meetings. We figured we would pull stunts later as well, but the focus was on the speaker presenting. Between the eight of us we had racked up seven absences last week, but none of us had actually missed a day. It was so helpful to have a sub to share around that we could just leave our students unattended whenever we wanted. Once I had even done so just to go to the bathroom at home instead of at school. It was amazing. There had been a student taking a make-up test in the lounge where the staff bathroom was, and I thought I'd just head home instead.

We weren't always the easiest to sub for since we weren't making full lesson plans all of the time, so we bought gift cards for the subs. The sub that had been in for me the first day of chaos had not returned, but the rest seemed happy to return. Today we definitely put both to work as we all were light on plans. I think Emily had the students pretending to text each other in Spanish and then design a snapchat filter set of instructions as well. I had the students making review posters and had passed out the standards from the typical end of unit. There were quite a few holes in them because I had stopped following my typical lesson sequence, so there were an overwhelming amount of questions from the students. I left those for the substitute to handle, and I was in with Diane most of the day. She had students designing an experiment to test how frictional force was affected by something and to construct a whiteboard with claim, evidence and reasoning. They were also on their own as Diane had set up where they could pay her 1% of their test score to ask a question. You could tell the students were torn but also were skeptical they would get much help if they did ask.

We started by calling the district office and asking who we could talk to about how to file a Freedom of Information Act request. They put us through to someone who told us what we would need and she offered to help us with creating the request so that it could be done cheaper and quicker. I told her that all we wanted to know were the financial details and to read the communications with the speaker that was presenting tomorrow. "Oh, that's all you want, I can send you that right now," she told us. The emails started arriving in Diane's inbox as we talked and she forwarded us the contract information as well. The district was paying $3200 as well as covering flight, hotels and other expenses. The total bill was over five thousand for all of the expenses and the presenter was relying on the district to provide technology assistance. Diane forwarded all of the information to the other team members.

Josh replied immediately and pointed out that one of the emails outlined the expectations for the presentation that it should include "differentiated instruction that all teachers can use." The irony of expecting differentiation that is the same for every teacher in different subject areas was not lost on us. The expectations and planning were brief and filled with educational buzzwords like "rigorous formative assessment strategies" and "interdisciplinary cultural proficiency." "I hate when people use the word rigorous when they mean challenging," I told Diane. "It's not even close to the same thing and educational experts should know their vocabulary." Christine replied to the group to point out that the contract included a clause that noted that there was not any data to support the practices being delivered to teachers. So basically, there was no empirical evidence to support any methods.

Diane and I spent the next two hours dissecting the emails and planning things we could do to interrupt the presentation. We had many interruptions so it was slow work but we were focused and came up with an organized system of possibilities that could easily be communicated between the four pairs of teachers. We also planned out our seats for the auditorium so that administration would not easily be able to reach us if they desired.

At lunch the other six joined us in Diane's room and we showed them what we had planned. Then we speculated what the rest of the day might entail and added a few more possibilities to our list. At this point, we had a lot of ideas that were flexible depending on how the set up and structure of the presentation was. We also were ready for some mischief in the staff meetings that followed as well. We figured there would be time to revise our goals in groups and that we would probably do some icebreakers that everyone would hate. We assumed that part of the meeting would take place in the library so David got to work putting together some audio clips that we could push through the speakers from his laptop. We also made some calls to local restaurants about lunch.

As lunch ended, I remembered the video I had posted and made sure to remind my final two classes that they were required to watch it for homework. Students asked a lot of questions about the video, and I had to disappoint them ahead of time by making sure they knew that the new video did not include any White Jesus. This one was strictly about learning and

I wrote there would be a quiz on the video Wednesday to make sure they learned everything. I actually had made a quiz in Spanglish to go along with the video. If I could hold my facial expression while passing it out, it was going to be amazing. One of the multiple-choice questions was:

#3 Qué tipo de video es señor Miles?
    A. Inteligente y guapo
    B. Demasiado alto
    C. Sí
    D. Todo el mundo de química

After school Diane and I both ran practice. We did a shorter loop and then some speed work. The short loop was out to the main road but then quickly into the neighborhood that wrapped around the school. So we ended up on the opposite side of the school and ran in towards the track. Then we did four 400-meter up tempo runs with short breaks in between. "The third one is the hardest. You're tired, but you're not close enough to taste the finish yet," I explained after the second lap. "The last lap you're tired but you can see the end, the victory, but it's before you get to that point where champions are made." That might apply to our competition pretty well too. When we finally got to the point where firings were going to come through things might get easier. But we were at the beginning of the workout and the end was not in sight.

Chapter 12 Professional Development

We woke up a bit early and met for coffee and breakfast. The start time was 8am, so we had extra time. Our normal start time was 7:10 am and we had to set up our classes. We took a lengthy breakfast and then arrived by 7:40 to pick out the best seating arrangements. We were in a large auditorium and the speaker and crew were setting the stage. The auditorium had a large stage and the center section of seats was very long. There were aisles on both sides and two small sections on the outside of the aisles. Above the back rows was a large balcony. The seats were dark blue so the seating was very dark, especially when the lighting was focused on the stage. There were no teachers present and a few administrators were scrambling around the room. We split up into pairs. Diane and Mary sat down left of the middle of the row about twelve rows from the stage. Josh and I sat down about ten rows back from them and about fifteen seats to the right to be just right of the middle. Christine and Emily sat back about twenty rows behind Diane and Mary and David and Darnell were about eight rows left of Josh and myself and three rows forward. As the crowd started filling in, we became surrounded by teachers and other staff. By 8am a large number of teachers were standing around chatting and the presenter wasn't even trying to start. The administration was just standing around.

Five minutes later the superintendent stepped up to the microphone and started to ask everyone to have a seat so that we could begin. A few did, but the roar of teachers chatting was not affected very much. After a minute went by, one of the superintendents of instruction went to the microphone and said, "If you can hear me clap once." Many of the elementary teachers clapped once. A couple of others did. "If you can hear me clap twice." More teachers, but not half of the teachers, clapped twice. The noise had died down considerably but was not gone. The superintendent talked over them and introduced the speaker. He had a large list of qualifications and had written a book with a witty title. Everyone applauded politely as the speaker enthusiastically ran to the microphone to start.

He was dressed in a fancy but comfortable sweater with slacks and running shoes. He had highly groomed facial hair and wore thin spectacles. He started with lame comments that always get laughter out of teachers. Things about drinking coffee and blaming things on parents. The crowd had settled in and a big giant PowerPoint presentation behind him had pictures of students smiling in a classroom. The speaker questioned the teachers. "We all know what we want, so how do we get it? How do we get happy students that learn and grow?"

All of a sudden, an extremely loud and aggressive Mary yelled out, "HEY!!!!" Her proclamation was loud and impossible to ignore. She stood up revealing her shirt that spelled out Be NiCe with periodic table elements, and had her hand raised. The speaker was clearly flummoxed.

"Yes?" he stammered.

"Can I go to the bathroom or what?" Mary asked loudly without the original urgency.

The speaker laughed, "Sure, go ahead."

"THANKS!" Mary shouted and then started to say excuse me loudly as she slowly made her way down the aisle. The speaker had completely lost his train of thought, and even though he thought he had handled the situation decently, the crowd started to giggle and talk about how their own students often derailed them with minutia like this all of the time. It was fun to see how a speaker would handle it.

"I apologize, I had lost my train of thought," the speaker eventually said trying to quiet the growing noise in the crowd. "Anyways, we all want the same things, so let's see what we can do to help you get there." A phone started ringing. It was just a straight up ringtone, and it was loud. It was coming from nearby Emily and Christine. The speaker at first paused, couldn't determine where the noise was coming from and started to try and talk over the ringing. As the speaker would try and start speaking again the phone would ring. He was visibly annoyed. Then he took a moment, regained his composure and said, "Good thing my phone didn't go off, my ringtone is mildly embarrassing." The crowd laughed a little bit and lots of tiny conversations were going on.

"So as I was saying," the speaker tried again, "what do we do for our students and should it be the same for the top students as the struggling students?" Mary returned and started back down the aisle to her seat. You could see the speaker look in her direction and pause.

"My bad!" Mary shouted. Quite a few teachers started giggling. We had all had this happen in our classrooms at some point where the best laid plans go to junk because a student felt the need to announce their bathroom intentions in the most disruptive manner possible.

"Let's take a look at some teachers and how they're managing the different learning styles in their classrooms." He flipped to a slide with a teacher lecturing on one side and on the other was a teacher sitting in a circle discussion. "Now what do we see here?" he asked. "One teacher is doing the same thing for the entire group and the other is differentiating their instruction."

"I disagree," Darnell interrupted while standing up. "Both of those teachers aren't differentiating but one is using better teaching methods than the other."

"Exactly," the speaker interrupted back. "This teacher is using methods that give them flexibility to reach different students."

"No," Darnell responded. I turned around to watch him as he shouted towards the stage. "You can't infer that from those pictures. And based on your writing about learning styles, which aren't evidenced based, we shouldn't be trusting your current set of comments on educational research."

"Yeah!" Diane shouted from the center in agreement. "Is it true that you only taught in the classroom for three years in one school? What gives you the right to speak down to us with approaches that aren't evidenced based!" The crowd grew uncomfortable. You could see Donna moving in the aisle on the side of the auditorium sizing up whether she would be able to go remove Diane from the auditorium.

David started shouting from next to Darnell, "If we're paying five thousand dollars for you to lecture at us about not lecturing, shouldn't we expect you to at least be knowledgeable about current research? And why aren't you differentiating in your presentation to all of the various content groups present here right now?"

"Look this isn't a Q and A format here. If you'd like to ask questions at the end, I'd be happy to stay after but this isn't going to be productive," the speaker tried to redirect.

Some random teacher that none of us recognized shouted out, "If you can't handle someone getting up to go to the bathroom, a phone ringing or some basic questions how are we supposed to trust anything you're about to say? Those things happen daily in our classrooms, and we all manage it."

"She's right!" I shouted. A lot of teacher grumbling built up.

"Look, I still get paid whether you listen or not," the teacher directed at the audience. "I can share with you what I know, or I can stand here and look pretty." The last three words were barely audible as the microphone had quit. The speaker tapped on the microphone a couple of times and looked to the sidelines with a look that was seeking help beyond the microphone.

The superintendent rushed onto the stage. "I'm sorry everyone, but let's take a quick five-minute break while we fix the sound equipment." The auditorium roared with noise as teachers got out of their seats and started marveling at the responses from the audience. A palpable excitement was present and very few teachers left to go to the bathroom or get coffee because many teachers had dreamed of shouting things out like this but never had the gall to follow through with it. They all wanted to see what would happen next.

The microphone was quickly "fixed" and the speaker pushed ahead to a slide that I assumed he was hoping would calm down the audience. It showed a student crying and a teacher consoling them. "Let's get started in one minute," the speaker said with a slight hint of dread in his voice. An audible "let's not" came from the balcony. The speaker ignored it and used his laser pointer to draw our attention to the slide. "How do we approach our struggling students? What systems do we have in place for them? What toll does having incomplete systems have on our teachers as we work to support these students? All of these questions require complex answers. I wish there was a magic wand that would make these concerns float away and you would have classrooms with 26 well behaved and academically successful students."

"Try 36!" a different balcony teacher erupted.

"I hear you," the speaker acknowledged. The auditorium immediately filled with quiet murmurs as many teachers doubted the validity of that statement.

The speaker continued with a slight increase in volume, "So what do we do when we get to classes with 36 students that have 36 different needs? How do we organize our approaches without sacrificing rigor for our top students?"

I turned to Josh, "I hate when people misuse the word rigor. He means challenging, and rigor is completely different." I got a text. I checked and Diane had sent me "Rigor? Don't lose it over there!" with a laughing face emoji. I showed Josh and he laughed.

The speaker had continued on while I performed my mini-tantrum. He had switched to a slide showing data for a school that had focused on differentiation as their goal and how the achievement had increased. Josh took a turn interrupting. "Excuse me, but on the public contract that you signed with our district the language specified that you did not have valid evidence of any methods. Is this fake data?"

The speaker rushed trying to hide something and quickly stated, "This is a simulated situation from another school."

His words were not missed though and yet another teacher in the balcony shouted, "Great, I'll just simulate my data for my evaluation and goals!" As the third comment from the balcony rained down, you saw a small group of administrators move towards the stairs to go monitor. I noticed that Donna had tried to move close to Diane but Diane had a small crowd surrounding her and Mary that prevented her from getting close enough.

The speaker was now rambling on about ways to differentiate in the classroom. He had a slide with things like change assessments for students, vary instructional methods and allow students to express themselves. David had thrown a half-filled bottle of water into the air and it landed on the ground. He had moved into the segment where he was playing bottle flip. The speaker told him to please stop. David shouted back, "This is how our high school students express themselves. I'm differentiating!"

The audience laughed and a few started applauding. I think I heard someone near the back say, "I hate that bottle flipping crap." I was surprised at how many teachers had joined in the fun without being in our planning. The auditorium gave them just enough privacy to be daring and challenge the presentation. This was unexpected and fantastic, but I worried that Diane and I were losing the credit for breaking down the speaker. I'd have to find my spot to jump in and the speaker was fading fast.

The speaker called for us to have a ten-minute break. We had already had the five-minute equipment issue, started about eight minutes late and it was not even 9am yet. Clearly we were winning. Teachers started moving around and were energized by those that had challenged the useless professional development. Teachers get stuck in these things, and the sessions can be unbearable and very insulting. This person offered us nothing useful, nothing to challenge or advise our specific teaching assignments, and yet he was getting a large sum of money while we were being told that our district was too low on funds to pay us our proper salary schedules. People were thrilled that he was being taken to task on his vague comments filled with educational buzzwords and jargon. But the speaker was not there when the break concluded. It was the superintendent, and she was not happy.

"Ladies and gentlemen, please sit for a moment," she started. The crowd got very quiet and sat quicker than I have ever seen teachers organize. "This morning we arranged for this speaker to come share with you some teaching strategies. I find the reaction to this disturbing and unprofessional. We are going to continue with the presentation but there will be no more outbursts or interruptions from the crowd. I am embarrassed by the lack of basic manners."

I decided this was my time to take control back. "Hang on a second," I shouted. The superintendent was shocked that anyone had spoken in the midst of her speech. "You know what I find rude? That we can find five thousand dollars for this crew to come share a bunch of educational buzzwords with us that produce no discernible improvement in anyone's teaching, but we haven't had the money to give teachers a cost of living raises in over a decade. There will be no difference in my teaching tomorrow whether I hear this presentation or not because this is bad PD and having to pretend like it's not a complete failure is not rude, it's us sticking up for our students that deserve better!"

At this point Donna had crawled over twenty teachers and had reached me. "Outside, now!" she glared at me. The crowd was silenced by my boldness and fear of retribution from the administration. But I saw several thumbs up on my long trek across the aisle to get to the exit. When I got about ten seats from the end of the row, I heard the same phone ring that had rung earlier at the start of the presentation. All kinds of giggling and commotion broke out, but instantly disappeared as the superintendent looked ready to find a second teacher to make an example of.

"What the hell were you thinking in there?" Donna started yelling at me.

"What is a single thing I said in there that was factually incorrect?" I challenged back. I might feel bad for putting Donna in a bad spot, but I felt highly justified in my comments. That presentation was predictably bad.

"It doesn't matter if you're right or wrong, you should not be challenging the superintendent in front of the entire district!" Donna countered. The superintendent was walking up behind me to yell at me herself.

"Oh, I'm sorry," I said with heavy sarcasm. "I forgot that I'm just a teacher and God forbid I have an opinion about teaching. I didn't mean to step on the toes of the real jobs that you guys have." I used air quotes when I said "just a teacher" and "real jobs."

The superintendent had been standing behind me listening and now she jumped into the mix. "You damn well know the difference between expressing your opinion as a teacher and intentionally undermining a presentation to a district full of teachers. Or did you miss that lesson because you were farting under your desk?"

"I'll tell you what," I responded angrily, "you want me to be polite, I will gladly go apologize in front of the entire district if you tell me one useful thing that's about to come out of the second half of that presentation. And to be clear my medical issues are none of your business because you can't afford to pay me proper health insurance because we're dropping money on the mess inside. It's not like I'm the only one speaking my mind in there; clearly it's a massive flop."

You could see the superintendent ready to explode but also cautious because I had brought up a medical condition, which would have made her way out of line. Donna took the opportunity to jump in. "Scott, go to your classroom. Helen and I will discuss what is going to happen next, but it's only going to get worse the more you speak. I will be there after the presentation concludes."

I scowled and then walked away determined. I thought about uttering something on the way back to have the final word but I decided against it. I had done a good job pushing back without being insubordinate. The goal had been to undermine the presentation and get the credit to one of us eight, and that had been accomplished. The superintendent being involved made things even more likely to progress to firing. It was going to be hard to sit in my room for an hour to wait and hear if Diane had done anything else to add on.

Before I could hear from her though, it was Donna that showed up first. "Scott, do you want to have a union person present with you for this meeting?" she asked. Wow, I thought. She was bringing out the big guns. Maybe I had won.

"I can handle myself," I replied calmly.

"The superintendent is going to be issuing discipline for multiple teachers involved in the presentation fiasco. You are one of them. You're going to get a second letter in your file. You will also be getting a one-day suspension with pay. If you wish to challenge this you can speak with your union representative, but it is unlikely to change. I will have to process this through the union, but you should anticipate having tomorrow off."

I couldn't believe it. What a wimpy punishment! I had mouthed off to the superintendent after her watching me hide under my desk for an uncomfortable period of time and then farting. And they were giving me a day off? Donna left, and I called to meet up with everyone else. They were on their way to my room they said. But then only six showed up a minute later. Diane was delayed.

"She stopped to talk with Donna, but she should be here any second," David told me.

"How about that presentation though?" I asked. "That was pretty amazing."

"It calmed down mostly after you left," Darnell admitted. "We tried doing another round of phone ringing, but so few people were paying attention that it wasn't very noticeable."

Diane walked in. We all stopped and looked at her. She started explaining, "I stopped Donna to ask her about what happened. She started to go after my behavior, but I interrupted her and told her to stop being so paranoid. She was a bit surprised, but I hadn't done much in the meeting so I wasn't going to get lectured about it. I shifted the topic back to Scott. She said that I would have to ask you about what happened in your meeting. So I asked if you were fired. She laughed. She was incredulous about the idea that you would be fired. She told me she still has not found a math teacher replacement yet, and she wasn't sure if she could fire any teacher in this hiring environment. She said even the superintendent told her to make sure to discipline you but not to push you away to another district."

"Wow," I said. "She told me I'm suspended with pay for one day and that I am getting a second letter put on file about my behavior. Then she left."

"Worth it!" Josh exclaimed.

"Right, even if we weren't trying to get fired, I would gladly take that deal," I agreed. "That meeting was legendary." We fist bumped.

"After you left it turned back to normal until the very end. As the presenter wrapped up the

179

presentation it was deathly quiet and then a couple of teachers gave a polite applause. But then people started shouting."

"That sure was worth two hours of my time!"

"Best five thousand bucks ever spent!"

"Why can't we get a decent presenter?"

"It got ugly and then people started booing," Mary described. "As people left the mocking of the presenter was downright cruel. He was off the stage before any of that happened, and I think I heard a car peel out in the parking lot."

"They cut a bit early and said we could take a longer lunch," Darnell said. "I think they were worried about jumping into another bad activity with so many riled up teachers. They gave us lunch to cool off."

Diane smiled and said, "And that will have to be where I catch up to Scott."

"I look forward to that," I admitted. "But just so you know, I may have told an irate superintendent that I would apologize if anything productive were to come out of the second half of the presentation."

"I have some plans," Diane smiled. "But you did good kid. Let's go get some lunch." I hadn't realized it, but I was hungry. I packed up briefly and we drove to go eat at a diner. I celebrated by having a brownie sundae for lunch, and it tasted as good as I thought it would. We came up with a list of professional development activities we had done in the past that we wished we could go back and heckle.

"Do you remember the one where they tried to get us to do an icebreaker in the auditorium that just didn't work?" Josh recalled.

"The one I want to go back and share my true feelings about was the one about the three-step process for discipline where each step had three components," David articulated. "I have 167 students. If you want a nine-step discipline process I'm going to need about half that many to be able to still have time to teach."

"Any meeting about goals would be mine," Mary admitted. "I work hard, and these goal settings are outrageous. It's like if we don't have their goal in our heads, we're bad teachers and we need to spend twenty hours a year feeling bad about having alternative goals for improving our teaching."

"Well we should have our opportunity for that," I suggested. Diane smiled. I could tell she had some ideas.

"I think you are all underestimating how terrible ice breakers are," Josh continued. "I heard one teacher say that they had to do one once where people got into groups of three, then one laid on top of the other while the third was to be rebirthed between them. Rebirthed!"

"That's not good, but if they try that today, I have several ideas on how to get fired," I commented.

"You have to keep your pants on Miles. It's not that kind of party," Emily replied.

"You and your rules," I said in a condescending voice. We wrapped up lunch and left an extremely generous tip. Just the extra petty cash we'd gotten from Josh went a really long way since our spouses and families couldn't know about our winnings. We didn't go too far over the line so that we would arouse suspicion, but throwing an extra twenty bucks for a tip was nothing at this point. We drove back in two cars to the school to get ready for our after-lunch meeting.

Chapter 13 Staff Meeting

The meeting started off with a surprise. Eric was supposed to be running the show, except he wasn't. Diane was! She started by passing out postcards to everyone and then announced that she was going to be starting us off with an icebreaker. Josh groaned. I remained intrigued.

"Ladies and gentleman, part of teaching is to have trust. You need to trust students to be perfect and trust in systems that can break your spirits. In order to build trust, we're going to have a ten-minute challenge of trust. There was a knock at the door. A delivery person walked in with Chinese food.

"I'm so sorry for interrupting," he said to Diane as she approached to take the food from him. She handed him some cash and told him not to worry about it.

Then as he got the food out from the bag Diane yelled, "TRUST FALL!" and she turned back to the delivery person and started dropping to the ground fast like she had passed out. The delivery person panicked and dropped all of the food. It went flying in all directions as he tried to catch Diane before she got a concussion landing on the hard floor. I noticed that Mary had been filming this entire time.

Diane stood up like the whole thing had been no big deal. The delivery person started to apologize for the food but Diane told him everything looked perfect and for him not to worry about it. He left and Diane turned to face the crowd with a big smile on her face. "You have ten minutes in your group to go around anywhere in school, find someone that you trust and do a trust fall while someone else records it. Then you can upload your video to our school's site and we'll pick the best one. Mary and I just got that one. Form a group and go ahead and get started."

Nobody moved. We were all stunned that she had just wasted at least thirty bucks of food for that stunt and also how nonchalant she had been the whole time. Then all of a sudden, I hear "TRUST FALL!!!!" Josh had quietly snuck onto the table and was falling expecting me to catch him. I jumped up from my chair and did what I could to stop him from dying. He fell with no regard for his safety. The chairs we were by fell over and a chunk of one splintered off because of how quickly I jumped up.

"Remember," Diane reminded us. "It must be recorded to count. Otherwise, very well done, Josh. Keep up the good work. Way to trust," she paused, "the process." Slowly the teachers got up awkwardly and started forming groups. A couple jokingly started to fall but didn't commit and didn't get close enough to anyone to be caught. Diane did not seem fazed by the lack of participation and she had a countdown clock running with eight minutes left. I started talking with Josh in the corner of the room away from the others.

"How did Diane get to be in charge of part of the meeting?" I asked.

"I'm not sure. Eric is pretty busy though, so I bet he was happy to let go of this," Josh responded. "I wonder what else she's going to do."

Emily and Christine joined us. "Trust fall," Emily shouted and then didn't fall.

"Weak," Josh assessed her.

"Jelly much?" Emily replied. A few of the teachers had headed into the hallway to meander and search for unsuspecting victims. But the school was mostly empty and there wasn't time to order food to be delivered. We walked back into the room and sat down as the time was about up. Diane was placing envelopes at each table, one per seat. Eric had begun doing work on his computer until it was his time. Apparently, he was either fine with trust falls or just didn't care enough to divert.

"Ok, let's get started," Diane announced as we sat back down. The timer had gone off with a pleasant-sounding alarm. "Did anyone get the chance to upload?" Diane checked the website, which had two videos posted. One was a teacher in the hallway that was about as interesting as the morning presentation. The other was Diane again. She was standing by a corner of a hallway in a school. Another teacher can be seen coming around the corner with her arms filled with papers to grade. Then you hear Diane yell "Trust Fall" and the papers flew everywhere as Diane just crashes into this poor soul. It had been an awkward presentation so far, but this video sent us into hysterics.

"Let's talk about trust," Diane continued as we slowly calmed back down. "What is trust and how do we get consistent above average trust? What I want us to think about today is what might you be doing

185

that you should be more trusting of and what should we not be trusting of. Everyone should have an envelope at their table. Inside is a postcard that later we are going to write to students that we might identify as below average. Our goal here is to increase trust and build relationships, so we are going to differentiate these students. I opened up the envelope and checked the postcard. It read:

Dear Below Average Student,

If you worked a bit harder, maybe I wouldn't have to sit through another dumb meeting where an administrator doesn't understand why there will never not be half of students that are below average. But that probably won't happen because instead of paying our teachers better, we are spending a large amount of money on questionable purchases that you can find listed on the back of this postcard. So good luck and remember, we're all cheering for you.

On the back of the postcard was a list of things the district had budgeted for and spent money on. But there was also a calculation showing how much money we spent on our annual goals. The calculations were extensive. They showed the average salary for teachers and administrators. They then estimated the amount of time wasted and converted everything into a final dollar amount. A few other teachers had been curious to check and discovered a true masterful lesson in pettiness.

"I'm going to turn this over to Eric in a little bit, but if you get bored during our ninth meeting about goals this year, instead of cruising your cell phone, send a message to a student that could use it." Diane finished speaking and sat down smiling. As she sat down, a teacher at her table showed her the postcard while laughing. Eric moved his PowerPoint onto the screen and got up to start his portion completely oblivious to what the postcards said.

"Thanks Diane," he acknowledged her. He looked exhausted. Our administrators had way too much work to do. "So today we're going to be looking at some different lessons that the district has put together and rate the lesson on how well it works for below average students and above average students to work on closing that gap."

Josh leaned over to me and quietly whispered, "No matter how many times they try and say that professionally, I'm never going to get over the stupidity of this whole thing." I nodded in agreement.

Eric had loaded a three-minute video clip. This one was a math teacher that put up a sample problem, let the students try to do a second question, and then started passing out a quiz before the video cut. Eric had conjured up a set of clickers so we could vote. For effectiveness for above average students the average score was 6.1 out of 10 and for below average students it was 3.2.

I raised my hand. Eric looked at me and nodded. "I'd like to counter the vote here," I explained. "I'd assume people are assuming that the below average students require more time to learn how to do the problem, but giving them a question that allows them to analyze their learning early is shown to be effective with cognitive science research."

"That's a fair point Scott. We'll just gather the data first though and then do some analysis after we've seen the results from all the lessons," Eric responded benevolently. Another video showed a science lesson where the teacher was doing a discussion. It scored high for both, but the teacher used way too many vocabulary terms and the lesson was a hot mess. They even used hot interchangeably with heat and temperature. I bit my tongue about the material in the lesson, but I was close to writing a postcard to the teacher after.

Josh leaned over again. "Are you thinking what I'm thinking?"

I looked at him with a blank look on my face. He explained quietly, "Just follow along." Then he stood up and walked right up to Eric who was looking at the slide with a laser pointer. I got up slowly and followed behind him.

"TRUST FALL!!!" Josh shouted before falling right into Eric.

"DOUBLE TRUST FALL!" I added with an enthusiastic collapse that resulted in a pile.

Diane took the opportunity and shouted, "Everybody trust fall!" and then about six teachers launched into a trust fall.

Eric was not thrilled. "Thanks everyone," he said in a muted tone. He ignored the preceding incidents and started to finish his presentation. Josh and I returned to our seats victoriously. Eric continued, "So what I'd like you to do now is to think about what lesson style was best and what you would add or change to that lesson to make it even better. Then we'll share in about three minutes."

"You know, if it weren't for the utterly ridiculous below average component of this, this would actually be a pretty good meeting for improving teaching," I noted. Emily and Christine agreed and we raised our hand to tell Eric who looked like he could use a compliment. Eric looked like he wasn't sure if it was worth it to be come over and hear what we had to say or if he should pretend like he couldn't see us. He eventually walked over with regret in his eyes.

As he walked up, I started to tell him, "Hey Eric, I think you know how we all feel about the average student thing, but the way we're doing this analysis is actually really great in my opinion. We're doing some quality thinking about things we do in teaching." Eric started to breathe again.

"I agree," Mary added on. "This I could do more frequently, and I really liked the examples you used."

"Great, I'm glad you're finding it useful," Eric said as he smiled a little bit. "If you'll excuse me though, I think I'm going to stand over there so I can escape if an entire teaching staff tries to trust fall on me." As we were talking with Eric, a few more teachers opened their envelopes and started spreading the joy of the postcards with their

189

seatmates. A wave of teachers reading them ensued as Eric unsuspectingly walked back to the front.

A teacher in a blue button-down shirt and red tie announced to the group, "Eric are these numbers accurate?"

"I don't know anything about what numbers you're talking about Sam," Eric responded. He walked closer to get a better look. His appearance shifted as he read the front and again as he read the back of the postcard. "Diane, can I speak with you outside for a moment?"

Diane hopped up and walked briskly into the hallway. We could all hear her say, "What's up?" in a tone that was slightly too much for the moment. Then an argument ensued that was covered up by the noise coming from the rest of the staff talking about the amount of money spent on goals.

I heard a teacher nearby tell someone, "You know, I never thought about how much money we waste on this stuff, but this is outrageous."

"And somehow we can't get enough funding for new furniture," another responded.

"You should see my chemistry supplies budget over the last ten years," I added with a thumbs down to indicate the direction my budget had moved in. The venting and complaining started up quickly and soon the entire room was filled with angry teachers that had just been reminded of all of the hits they had taken over the last few years. Soon Diane entered into the room and walked back to her seat. Eric walked in and I honestly couldn't tell if he was angry or exhausted.

He looked around at the room and he quickly became hesitant.

He walked back out to gather himself, got a drink of water and then came back ready to defend himself from our complaints. "Look," he stated. "I get your anger, and I share your anger. I do. I've had cuts just like you, and I get to see all your budget woes and I hate it. But this is required by the state for us to do, and there is no cheaper alternative."

"In lots of the neighboring districts they don't spend nearly as much effort or money on this," our band teacher Mr. Lee offered to the group in as polite a manner as he could. "Maybe this is something we should reconsider what we're getting out of it and what we're putting into it." At this point David played an applause sound effect from his computer that ran through the speakers. Eric looked confused and waited for the noise to die down. Most teachers looked around, a few were enthralled.

"I don't disagree with that, and I'll do my best to forward your feelings along," Eric agreed. Sometimes I marveled at how patient the administrators were. Although they probably got a significant amount of practice dealing with angry parents and other administrators that were less competent.

Josh gave one last effort at spinning the meeting out of control. "I get that you can forward that along, but what can we do in the immediacy to suspend these goals and come up with something that satisfies state law without destroying teacher ambition and costing loads of money?"

Several teachers nodded in agreement and a few muttered in support. Eric calmly responded, "I understand your frustration, and I'm going to do my best to be helpful. In the meantime, why don't we spend the rest of the afternoon doing two things. First I need you to meet in groups and compile your thoughts into this shared document. Then you can take the rest of the time as prep time to get ready for the rest of the week." That worked. Teachers had a bunch of work to do and quickly got their assignment done and either went back to their rooms to work or just went home to get grading done. I took advantage too and set up some plans for the next day as I served my suspension. I also had a couple of ideas, but I would need the next day to get them planned and ready by Thursday when I returned.

Chapter 14 Stability

  Wednesday I had been off. For the first time in my career, I had completely phoned it in and sent in a movie from the 1970s to watch. Thursday morning I came in really early, and I was on a mission. Josh made the early trek in as well because it was going to take more than just me to get things situated. We lugged all of the equipment in from the car before anyone else had arrived so nobody saw anything. Then we locked my door and got to work assembling. By about twelve minutes before the start of school, we were ready. We had assembled a full-size trampoline complete with net. I got out some squishy soccer balls to throw in the middle. I had measured Tuesday before I left, and we had about 8 feet of clearance. The lab ceiling was pretty high for some reason, so even though a trampoline violated everything in my science teacher body for lab safety, it was incredibly fun. We spent the final couple of minutes arranging some stools around the trampoline since the entire class would be unlikely to fit on at the same time. Then we opened the door.

  "Is this serious?" Sydney asked as she walked in. She immediately took off her shoes and started jumping. The kids had to duck slightly to avoid bumping their heads but the trampoline was legit. As a couple more students entered it got noisier and Diane poked her head in to see what was going on.

  "Well I'm glad you at least did the fireworks lesson and trampoline day on different days," she commented.

"I moved all glassware and chemicals out of the lab and did a full clean up before I left on Tuesday," I justified myself. Even though we were trying to stretch things to get fired, I did feel judged by a fellow science teacher.

"Hah!" exclaimed Matt. He had found the teeter totter that I had brought in as a pair of seats. He and another student started playing. I always enjoyed watching high school students enjoy playing with things from early elementary school. As the bell rang, I instructed students to either sit on the trampoline while remaining still or to join the stools around the trampoline. I was just starting into the lesson when a PA announcement happened.

It was David again. "Please excuse this interruption, but there is a package at the front office for a Captain McSwag! Captain McSwag please come to the front office for a package." Next thing you know Diane burst in and announced to my class, "If anyone needs me, I'm going to be picking up my package." She then showed off an over-sized ID that read Captain McSwag and had her picture on it. She triumphantly walked out of class and headed to the office. We all cracked up. I rolled off of the trampoline and checked in on her class. Not only were they still laughing about the announcement and their teacher's involvement, but they had a new learning tool in their class.

At the center of the front of the room was a giant spinny wheel. It had spokes to slowly stop the wheel from spinning like one of those wheels on a board game. The wheel was split up into at least a dozen sections in a variety of colors. I gave it a spin and it whirled around for about fifteen seconds before slowing down and clinking to a stop. It stopped on a blue triangle that said "Why are you the way that you are?"

"That seems a bit harsh," I proclaimed as the students laughed. "It doesn't even know me, and I'm already being judged."

"That's our new physics wheel of judgement," one of the students in a blue hoodie explained. "We use it a lot."

"The other day Byron had to use it because he didn't complete his homework," a very happy student wearing a pink t-shirt explained.

I looked at the student in pink and said, "On Wednesdays we wear pink!" They looked confused so I then whispered, "On Wednesdays..." They made an awkward glance to the left indicating they still didn't get it.

The student next to them leaned over and said, "It's Thursday, not Wednesday. One more time and you're going to need to spin." The student in pink jumped up and spun the wheel completely unafraid. The wheel spun around for a bit and then slowly settled onto a white segment that said "Your parents emailed your teachers to tell us that they don't even like you and they aren't proud of you."

"Harsh," I said in awe of the wheel. I then turned towards the other students, "but accurate also." I headed back to the door and Diane was walking in with a large box. "I'll get that door Captain McSwag!" I announced boldly and then held the door.

Diane looked at me like I was a weirdo and then said, "Why are you the way that you are?" Her class erupted into cheers, and I left with my head hanging low. I had somehow completely forgotten that next door Josh and I had built a trampoline, but I heard jumping happening and I quickly made my way back in. It was somewhat wild.

"Hey settle down!" I pretended to be upset that students were being wild in the trampoline room. The students quickly settled down. I took off my shoes and jumped into the ring. Most of us sat down with our feet crossed but it was hard to not fall over. There were a lot of us on the trampoline, so it was sloped downwards, and we all gradually shifted towards the middle.

"Let's talk about stability," I started. "Are we stable on this trampoline?"

"Nope," John admitted, and then he rolled onto his side to demonstrate.

"So what is it like when we have unstable chemicals?" I asked the group. I paused and let them soak in this moment with absurdness yet also high levels of cognitive science dual coding going on. "What are some chemicals that you know of that we would consider unstable?"

A student named Emily raised her hand and the shift caused everyone around them to have to adjust their torsos slightly. "I would say stuff that lights on fire," Emily responded.

"Right, which is why we are now going to put flammable chemicals under the trampoline to show what happens when we mix unstable chemicals with unstable trampolines," I said while getting up to go grab something from the fume hood. Students quickly started shuffling under the netting to get out of the trampoline. "I'm kidding," I admitted. "I'm not going to light any of you on fire. I'm not going through that paperwork again."

"Why do you have to do so much paperwork about lighting students on fire?" Drake asked me.

"I don't, I was just lying," I said and then shifted my eyes around suspiciously. "Ok, let's talk more about the trampoline. What are the chemicals like that it is made out of?"

"Stretchy," Drake responded.

"How do you envision that working?" I asked back. "What makes a chemical stretchy at the particle level? Do the particles themselves stretch and get longer and shorter?"

"No," Mike responded quickly. I acted surprised.

"Ok then, what does happen?" I asked. "Talk to your neighbor and come up with what happens when you jump on a trampoline to the particles of the trampoline." The class burst into noise and some started jumping to demonstrate what they were saying. I let them talk for a couple of minutes and then decided to bring them all back together. "Now, let's make an important point. Regardless of how you explain how particles stretch, it's important to think critically about things you see chemicals do and wonder what does that look like at the small level. Because it might not be as simple as someone giving you a two-sentence explanation of what's happening. It might take you years of watching things to eventually understand it yourself. But it's worth the thinking because chemistry is amazing." Every student had stopped shifting or bouncing and was deep in thought. "Homework tonight: go home and find something in your house made out of chemicals and think about why those chemicals make that thing work the way that it does. Tomorrow we'll compare what you find with what everyone else finds. You have three minutes to play on the teeter totter and trampoline."

That more or less continued for the rest of the day. I brought in a trampoline like an idiot, but I also loved chemistry and it was surprisingly productive for discussion. The students were engaged every hour with a few moments of distractedness, but overall a lot of learning happened. At lunch, we met in my room because I had a trampoline. Diane, David, Darnell and Mary joined us and Diane wheeled in her spinny wheel. It had wheels!

"How long did that take to build?" I asked.

Mary explained, "We had the wheel done this weekend but the wheels needed Monday to finish it off. We snuck it in on Tuesday."

"I helped," David announced.

"You sure did pal," Darnell patted David on the head condescendingly. David grinned.

"Oh, I completely forgot during Monday's lunch," I remembered suddenly. "I have some emails to respond to from last week still."

Dear Mr. Miles,

We were disappointed in Robert's last score on his exam. He studies hard but is not improving. Do you have any recommendations?

Sincerely,
Mr. and Mrs. Dobby

"They named their son Bobby Dobby?" Diane asked. I nodded.

"This one I know what I wanted to write back; it's the others that I'm going to want help with."

Dear Dobbyies,
Sorry I did not respond to you right away, I had better things to do with my time. Robert's studying at home would be more effective if he were to work harder during class and learn more at school. He should already have instructions on how to do this. Thanks!
Scott

"Why are you the way that you are?" Diane asked me again.

"How did you know that I got that part of the spinny wheel?" I asked her.

Diane smirked and said, "That's for me to know and you to find out."

"How suspicious," I noted.

"Hey I had a thought," Darnell informed us.

"What was the occasion?" Josh interrupted him.

"Hah, very funny," Darnell replied dismissively. "Anyways, I was thinking we should make up a fake spirit week. We can post fliers in our classrooms and then spread it to all over the building for a fake spirit days. I can even submit an announcement and we'll say it's for a science club or something. But let's dress up like absolute weirdos. I'm thinking we do a pool floatie day."

"I vote parking cone day," David said immediately like this had been on his mind for some time.

"Favorite chemical element day?" I suggested nervously. There was no immediate reaction. I thought about making everyone else aware of my brilliant pun, but I hesitated too long.

"Let's do a Scrabble day, and we can all get letters that spell out a swear word," Diane recommended.

"That works," Darnell wrote down Scrabble day, but he had not written down any of the others.

"We should buy a laminating machine," Emily proposed. "I'd bet we could post all kind of signs all over the building that are hilarious if we laminated them first. We can even get a fake approval stamp."

"We should do a gladiator or medieval day, but then really go hard at it. Maybe hire a makeup artist and costume provider," Christine suggested.

"I know someone that could pull that off," Emily agreed. Darnell wrote down something again, but only one thing.

"We should hire the costume person every single day really," I added. "It's not like cost will be an issue."

"Well I'd like one to be pajama day so I can wear slippers and a bathrobe to work," Josh proposed. Darnell wrote that down again.

"Hey Darnell, what's wrong with favorite element day or parking cone day?" I asked aggressively.

"I'll put them on the maybe list. Let's think it over for a day and plan some costumes before we decide," Darnell responded like a politician.

"If we do parking cone day, I'm going to dress like a dog," Josh warned us. "So be ready for that to happen."

"Parking cone day is great because you're either a parking cone or you're not," David explained. "It's so simple that it can only go well." Christine looked at David like she thought he might be stupid.

"Well if we want this to happen next week we'd better get rolling because we'll need posters telling what day everything is up by tomorrow," Diane warned us.

"I'll pick the days, but I'll need help making posters and putting them up," Darnell offered.

"I'll contact the costume and makeup," Emily offered.

"I'll put together the announcement," Mary added.

"I'm going to find a way to get a stamp that is similar enough to the office approval one," David said.

"I'll help Darnell with the days and posters," Josh agreed.

"Diane and I can get a laminating machine and we'll also start looking for fun signs to post around the building," I said figuring that way we're doing something but it sounded like spirit days were covered. I turned to Diane, "Do you want to run practice today or go out and get the laminating machine?"

She responded, "You run practice since I did it yesterday; I'll get the machine. Then have the captains run practice tomorrow and we can tour the school looking for good opportunities for official looking signs."

We talked a little bit longer about some potential spirit days, but without any brilliant ideas. We also spent some time jumping on the trampoline because it was fun.

By the end of the day, we had our spirit week schedule and a rough draft of a poster ready. The beginning completely fabricated a science club run by Diane called Team Science and said they were doing a fundraiser for social awareness. The schedule would be:

Monday: Pajama day

Tuesday: Scrabble day
Wednesday: Medieval Warrior day
Thursday: Parking Cone day
Friday: Bear Shoulders day

We figured pajama day would take the least planning, so students would be able to pull that off. We also put Bear Shoulders day where you would make your shoulders like a bear, or other animal. That was a polite jab at our really lazy dress code policy that would discipline female students for bare shoulders as if the dress code wasn't already heavily slanted against the female students. It also allowed us a wide range of costume options. I had my own plan that I very much looked forward to for Friday.

I went to practice after school and ran six miles with the team. Diane went out and bought a new laminating machine. Then she and I walked around the school on Friday at lunch to search for places we could put up signs. The school layout was a big square where each side of the square had a parallel hallway that housed a group of classrooms. Our crew was all in one hallway except for Emily who was in the parallel portion of our side. The side opposite the front is where the athletic rooms, gym, pool and some of the band rooms were. Each hall had its own set of bathrooms and then, in the center of the school, is the cafeteria, the library and the auditorium. As much as I liked to complain about things, the layout of the school was functional and the design was beautiful.

"I feel like each hallway should get a sign that has a prohibited item that just doesn't make any sense at all," I suggested. "Like this one could say no dragons allowed due to incident, or please do not drive cars in reverse in this hallway."

"I like it," Diane agreed. "Maybe one could be please refrain from dancing, even if music happens."

"No brushing your teeth in between classes."

"Do not divide by zero."

"This bathroom is officially malaria free."

"Stop calling people Fred if that is not their name."

"If you're doing three push-ups, you might as well do eleven."

"If you don't know an answer to a test, make sure to stare at the test and feel bad about yourself for at least three minutes, you loser."

"Bottle flipping is stupid, and I hate you."

We went back and forth for quite a bit, throwing ideas out there and taking notes on the better ones. When we walked by a fire extinguisher I wrote down "For hot fires only, do not use on cold fires." When we walked by a big window Diane wrote down "Only let in sunlight during the day."

After school, we quickly stopped by practice to make sure that the captains knew the workout and that everyone was present. They were doing speed work, so the two captains alternated between running and timing. Diane and I started printing out signs and laminating them. For the No Dragons sign we printed a color picture of a big dragon with a big red circle with a line running across it. Some of the more aggressive signs we put in smaller print so that administration and other teachers might go longer without noticing them. I made a "Warning: May Contain Dihydrogen Monoxide" sign for the drinking fountain furthest from my room. Diane made a "If you jump, you are in zero-gravity, there is gravity in space, lots of it, it's a stupid word" sign for the athletics hallway where the mats for tumbling were. We all had our science things that drove us bonkers. We spent about an hour putting signs up, and the last one we set right at the front of the building, one that said "I'm not a therapist, I'm a sign, please stop talking to me!"

The other six had gone home to work on projects for next week or just to go home. Diane and I decided we would head out for a drink before going home. We went over to The Teacher's Lounge, and she ordered the rough draft, but I went with something lighter.

She started in, "So have you thought about what you're going to do when one of us gets fired soon?"

"A little, but not a lot. I think that it's honestly kind of hard to think about not teaching anymore. I always wondered what it would be like to do a different job, but I never expected to even switch careers, let alone retire at thirty-six."

"Well let me tell you, I am ready at age forty-nine. I am looking forward to this immensely. Although, I admit that the past two weeks have been the most fun that I've ever had. I'm so glad that at that meeting in Josh's room we all agreed to carry this out. I'm also glad that you and I are the head of the teams."

I started laughing. "I currently have a trampoline in my classroom. A legit full-sized trampoline. This is so much fun. Are you going to move?"

"I think so. I'll have to talk it over with my family. But I would think we would at least buy a new house if not a new location as well."

"I haven't thought about it much because I would want a lot of input from my family. It would be hard to move for me though. I moved a lot as a kid, and so my current house is a big deal to me because it's my home and I don't feel like I have any other one if that makes sense. My parents' house, they moved to after I was done with college, so I don't have a childhood connection to it."

"It's hard not talking to my family about it," Diane admitted. I agreed. I felt like at home I had to pretend like it hadn't happened so I didn't feel like a liar.

"Ok," I said changing the conversation. "What will you miss the most about teaching and what will you be the happiest to never do again?"

"I'll miss getting up in front of the class and teaching. Having a great discussion on physics, looking at an amazing demonstration, getting students to think hard about how things work. I will definitely miss that. Grading though, never having to grade again sounds beautiful. Oh, and not having to set an alarm clock for 5:04 am makes me so happy I could punch a person."

"I agree on all three. It's weird to think about not ever doing anything to teach chemistry again. I've spent so much time and effort becoming so good at explaining chemistry and getting students to think hard about chemistry. I just think about all of the books that I've read, and thinking that I've done and to just let that go even though I find it a rush to be in front of a class. It's weird." Our conversation paused as some of these thoughts were being shared for the first time with another person, and there was some emotion flowing that we had been hiding while we planned pranks and did goofy things at work. We would all be sad when this ended even though new things were coming that would also be amazing.

"I'm going to miss our group too," I finally broke the silence. "I figure that we'll have the means financially to see each other periodically, but I'd be lying if I weren't trying hard to appreciate this final run of teaching. I wonder how many of us will still be in Michigan next year."

"I've spent so many years working with Mary," Diane reminisced. "We've had a lot of lunches together." I had expected to go out and have fun coming up with funny ideas, but the emotions were hitting me fast, thinking about all of the big changes looming. It felt like I was about to lose such a big portion of who I was. The contest had helped me avoid thinking about it, and not telling anyone outside of our group helped me avoid it as well. But the more I thought about it, the more my nostalgia grew.

"Well this ended up being more depressing than I had anticipated," I said. Diane laughed. I laughed too. "Our signs were quality though."

"They really are great," Diane agreed. "Any fun plans for next week or do you need the weekend to catch up?"

"I have an idea that I'm working on the details for," I hinted.

"I have an idea that's big, but it might take me a bit to pull it off," Diane admitted.

"As soon as one of us gets fired, you know the next day we'll remember something that we always wanted to do and should have done," I anticipated. We talked for a bit longer about the funniest things we had done and some of the student reactions. Then we left to go see our families for the weekend. As I drove home, I left the music off and just thought about all of the things I had felt. I even started talking out loud a bit about the things I would miss the most. When I got home, I sat in my car for a minute by myself before heading in.

Chapter 15 Spirit Week

It was pajama day. I had a robe, sweatpants and a t-shirt on. I didn't even care if it did nothing to help the cause, I was going to enjoy wearing comfortable clothes at school. I did this every time we had spirit weeks with pajama day. I was not alone in my endeavors to be warm and fuzzy at school. Emily had dinosaur slippers that made roaring noises when she walked. David had taken things slightly further and had dressed in similar apparel but had added a few accessories. He had a cardboard sign that read "Will teach for food, extra credit for $$$" and had dressed like he was begging for change. He then proceeded to literally fall asleep on the ground outside of his classroom. I guess I can't know for sure that he actually fell asleep and wasn't just pretending. But it was for long enough and it looked and sounded like he was asleep. I put a dollar into his cup. His cup had a lot of money in it.

Not many students had noticed the signs, but a few participated. We had spirit weeks so frequently that no one from administration seemed to think anything was out of the ordinary. But the few students and staff that did participate would push more to get involved in the upcoming days. During prep I had gotten an email from a parent.

Dear Mr. Miles,

I know that my daughter Sarah has been having a hard time in your class. I was hoping to get some thoughts on what could be done for her to do

better. She has a high grade in every class except for chemistry and she says that she doesn't get a lot of help during class.
Sincerely,
Mrs. Runyan

Dear Mrs. Runyan,
This was crazy but prior to today I had not been teaching anything at all. We had just been sitting around every day while kids either slept or socialized. But I think this may have been a massive mistake and starting tomorrow we're going to try doing learning instead. Thanks for the idea!

Scott Miles

After school, Diane was running practice, so I made a new YouTube video. This was without a script and without a costume, unless you count the robe. But the video was high quality. It started with a view of the interactive whiteboard with all kinds of chemical symbols on it. Then I stepped right in front of the camera. "Are you here to improve your chemistry? Well that was a terrible decision. If you wanted to become a faster runner would you watch someone run? Of course not! So watching me do chemistry isn't going to help you. In fact, it might actually leave you worse off because you'll become overconfident since I do all of the steps and explanations so easily. If you want to get better at chemistry, you have to think on your own. Write down what you think something is and then look at what you understand and what you don't know yet. Then use evidence and experiences and logic to build from what you know. And it should be hard and confusing. Learning chemistry isn't easy, so watching a video is not going to make you better. It's just going to comfort you, and you'll still be the same ignorant person after, but with ten fewer minutes to actually learn. Turn this video off and start learning on your own. Don't be lazy about your learning. No one can do your thinking for you."

It wasn't horribly controversial, but it was my truth and I felt ready to put it on camera and ship it out for students everywhere to see. When I had first started teaching, I tried hard to make the learning as simple as possible for the students, and I was always surprised at how little they learned. Gradually I figured out that the harder it was for students, the more they learned. I also felt a little bit like if I was out of teaching soon, I might as well leave behind some of the things that I had learned along the way for future students and teachers to see. I had a decent following on my channel.

Tuesday I was going to assign the video for homework and a one-page summary or reaction to it. I figured it would be a good chance to use some more grading stickers. But more importantly, it was Scrabble day. We had strategically made our scrabble letters in groups to make things a bit more ambiguous. I had made an element square for Boron. David, Darnell, Diane and Mary had gotten their letters made by the same place and spelled out THIS.

Emily, Christine and Josh got their letters made by a different place and spelled out LUL. A few other staff had made letter costumes as well, but between the eight of us we definitely took a class photo spelling out BULLSHIT. The mixed-up costumes gave us an out if we wanted to have one. Diane was the S in THIS, so she and I also walked around throughout the entire day as some BS. We may have induced quite a few posts on social media just by walking through the cafeteria. The office staff took a picture that they said they would work in somehow when the need arose.

Unfortunately, some students got in on our idea and also may have started making Scrabble letters by taping a piece of paper to their shirts and there were some unfortunate combinations made. Teaching was pretty fun that day. All day long I had B puns rolling. Be yourself, be calm, be patient, be prepared were happening more frequently than emails from parents upset about B grades on tests. I told all hours to BE ready for some homework and that there was a new video posted. At least two students per class immediately checked to see if it was another Chemistry with Jesus video. I looked forward to the comments on the video itself as well as from the students on paper.

At lunch we all ate together in my room. The trampoline made it a much more enjoyable social experience. We had cut back on our planning a bit relative to the first two weeks of the contest and a lot of our ideas we worked together on at this point and split the blame evenly. At one point we got a picture of

Diane, Darnell, David and Mary jumping on the trampoline and Josh yelled, "Don't get any shit on the trampoline!"

Wednesday we all went way overboard. Almost no one else participated but we were decked out from head to toe with elite warrior outfits. Our weapons were extremely toy looking with some bright orange so that we didn't for a second get into issues with that, but our makeup and costumes were on point. Josh looked legit like an orc. I was half horse and half warrior. We did fencing battles in between classes every hour while students cheered us on.

Meanwhile Diane and her group had come in early and constructed a giant barrier of cinder blocks in front of her classroom. Every hour students had to move the cinder blocks out of the way to get in and at the end of the hour they had to go reset them for the following hour. Every single class had multiple students, usually students on the lower end of the GPA curve, volunteering to move cinder blocks in and out of the way. During the first hour a student moved the entire wall by himself to use the bathroom. The best was when we helped because our costumes made the process even more hilarious. Darnell tried using his fake axe and Josh tried carrying blocks while riding on the centaur.

Then at lunch all eight of us went into the cafeteria and just sat down by groups of students we didn't know while staring off into space. They usually moved away. One daring student tried to poke Josh with his finger and Josh shifted suddenly and the student freaked out and fell over. It was a sad moment for nachos, but glorious for teachers and people that like seeing other people fall over. Christine had a really gruesome face done with makeup and she kept standing in the lunch line while staring blankly at the kid standing in front of her. It was low key terrifying.

In class we did a demonstration where I had reacted aluminum and iodine powders. This resulting in a glowing mass that gave off plumes of violet gas. I did a video of it after school before practice where I was still dressed as a centaur. The majority of the reaction was just the reaction, but there was an odd five seconds before and after where I walked up to initiate the reaction with a drop of water, and then I walked by the camera again at the end to shut everything down.

I decided to stick with it after school, and I ran in my costume and makeup. I did not go very far and I managed not to sweat, so when I was done, I still looked mostly the same. But quite a few of the cars I jogged past honked and slowed down. A couple grabbed a picture, I think. I didn't run as fast as normal but the team seemed to be a step faster today and had quite a distance between us. When I went home after, I edited the video. I left in the centaur parts, and I added some clippity clop sound effects before posting it online.

Seven of us dressed up as parking cones on Thursday. Over the weekend Josh had found a party store that made big giant parking cone costumes, and we bought seven. They were about 6 feet in height and besides being oversized looked exactly like a big orange parking cone. Josh held true and dressed as a big giant brown dog with floppy ears. Before school started, we met in the parking lot and blocked off the entrance. Then we moved to the parent drop off loop and split the loop into two lines. Both of those were short lived because the traffic was mildly terrifying. Parents were in a rush and our presence had no impact on their impatience. We also didn't want to wait too long in case police were called. The best thing we did was to walk up and down the stairs during passing periods. No one could get around us, and it was a chaotic mess. Just seven teachers as large parking cones saying, "Excuse me." We'd get stuck getting past each other so the students had no way around us. When we walked down the hallway, it was bad, but the stairs were even funnier. At lunch we made an obstacle course with the seven of us and a student timed Josh going through the seven cones on a loop. Then we headed to the lunchroom and stationed ourselves in different spots. Josh would then come close to one of us, smell us, start to lift his leg and we'd yell out, "NOPE, NOPE, NOPE!" Then we'd move away and he'd find a different cone. The lunchroom loved us. We found a pot hole in the floor by one table and I filled it in so no one would get hurt. Sometimes four of us would converge on a student slowly, and then at the last second, we'd rush in and surround them so they couldn't escape. At the end of lunch, a student shouted that we should joust, and so

215

Darnell and I ran towards each other and at the last second turned the cone tips in to collide. It caused us to spin from the collision and Darnell fell down and rolled over. Diane rushed over and blocked traffic for him.

During one of the afternoon passing periods Diane and I walked around as cones to see our signs in action. When we got to the one that said "If you're doing three push-ups, you might as well do eleven," we both started doing push-ups. Diane could get to eleven, but I was not built for push-ups. Around six I started to slow down significantly so the students in the hallway started counting for me. Each push up had a significant pause in between. When I got to nine, I fell down to the ground. The crowd let out a sound of disappointment. Then I burst into push up ten and they cheered. They started chanting "One more, one more," and I got stuck at the bottom until I felt assistance. Diane was pulling me up, and I pushed and did the eleventh push up. Then Diane and I high fived, and she even signed an autograph on a student's physics notebook.

During last hour, we all met in David's room for a picture and to congratulate David on his brilliant idea. No one thought it would be fun, and not a lot of people participated, but we weren't aiming for large turnout. We wanted to have fun and cone day delivered. The whole day had been a blast. At lunch even Eric and Donna had stopped by because they had heard about the commotion from Maurice and they were laughing heartily. It was nice to see the three of them smiling and having fun.

Friday was bear shoulder day. Our district had a dress code policy that said students may not have bare shoulders. The rationale was that it was too distracting for male students. It is a terribly policy. Dress code policies in schools give creepy staff the means to harass students. There are lots of appropriate outfits that involve bare shoulders. And the message behind the policy was that women should be responsible for avoiding inappropriate male attention. All eight of us were pretty pumped to bring some attention to this outdated policy. It had not been noticed by the administration, although it was quite possible that they also looked forward to the dress code being revised to something more reasonable. They had to deal with the aftermath of all of the drama.

Not only did the eight of us show up with some form of bear shoulders, but a lot of students participated as well. A lot of male students wore shirts without shoulder coverage and then drew bears on their shoulders to "cover" them. One student had sewed fake fur onto the shoulders of her shirt. A few were wearing sports teams that had the bears as the mascot. Mary had found a bear costume that went from head to toe. Darnell had also found a complete bear costume, but his had holes cut out in the arms and also the shoulders. So he had a bit of bare shoulders for his bear shoulders.

I, on the other hand, was the one teacher not wearing any sort of bear apparel. I had two big fish. One was on the left shoulder and the other on the right. Both fish had big giant hooks coming out of their mouths. If anyone asked me, I was sticking to the story that this was bear food shoulders. But I didn't fool Josh. He saw me as I walked into his classroom and started laughing. "Hooker wear?"

I smiled and responded, "I have no idea what you're talking about." There was a student holding a sign that had a big TWSS on it. "What's that about?" I asked Josh.

"Oh man," Josh replied. "That's our "That's what she said" sign. Whenever a student says that's what she said in the appropriate context they get to hold the sign until someone takes it from them."

"You've got to be kidding," I said incredulously.

"THAT'S WHAT SHE SAID!" Josh shouted. The kid holding the sign dropped his head and walked over and relinquished the sign.

"Thanks a lot," the kid said dryly towards me. I left Josh's room and headed over to Emily's room to tell her about the TWSS sign. Class had started but we had been in and out of our rooms all week.

Emily's class was all standing up and she was directing them in Spanish. It sounded like she was organizing them into groups based on the alphabet. As I walked to the front of the room, I realized she was having them choose seats based on their current grades. She saw me and paused. "Hey what's up?" she asked.

"I came to tell you about Josh's new sign," I replied. "Are you putting the students into groups based on their grades?"

"Not exactly," she responded. "I'm just having them stand up based on what their current grades are for no reason at all." I looked surprised. "I know, there really isn't any good explanation for this, but this class has been misbehaving all year, so I'm just doing this to be a bit of a jerk to them and also to get them to shut up and pay attention. It's worked pretty well actually." She then called out A and a chunk of students sat down. Then she called out B or B+ and more sat down. Eventually she was down to D and E. I let her get back to it and found my way back to my class finally.

My class was chatting about the dress code or just doing nothing. We started learning about the moles and we went outside to do some sidewalk chalk to figure out how many chalk atoms we left on the sidewalk. While most students were drawing, Matt asked me why I had fish on my shoulders. "It's food for bears," I said. Matt looked at me skeptically and went to go talk to his friends.

Later I saw Donna walking into Diane's room. Diane was on her prep period. I pretended to forget something and headed back to my room to eavesdrop. I had barely done anything to get into trouble this week and was curious to see what Diane had been up to. I walked into our storeroom to hear better.

Donna was asking Diane, "Well why are you taking photos of students in the first place? Why would you post them on the internet? Did you think making memes of your students would be funny?" I wasn't sure, but it sounded like Diane had been taking pictures of students that were sleeping and making fun of them using common memes.

Diane was now responding to the allegations. "I didn't post anything online, and I did not take any pictures of students. Students have been making these memes, not me. I had nothing to do with any of these things and don't appreciate the accusations."

Donna was not pleased and seemed tired of Diane. "Well, the email I received implies otherwise and I don't care who made the meme since it's proudly displayed in your room. And if you did create the meme, you'd better be ready to defend yourself." I heard Donna get up and walk out. I went outside to go make sure my class wasn't doing anything horrible outside. Donna stopped me as we crossed paths. "Scott, when is the event for your club that we had the spirit week for?"

"I had nothing to do with the spirit week," I lied. "I thought it was for Mary or Diane."

Donna's face perked up slightly when I mentioned Diane. "Oh, I thought you were the one putting up the posters and you were so involved in dressing up this week. Why do you have fish instead of bears on your shoulders? Bear food?"

I nodded. "Yep, fish for bears to eat. Actually, now that I think about it, I think it was that newer teacher that made the spirit week. Dave or something?" There was no new science teacher named Dave or new teacher that I knew of. I started leaving to go outside with my students. I turned back and looked over my shoulder. Donna was just standing there with an odd look on her face. Whatever she was thinking, it didn't look good for me or for Diane. It looked like she was thinking about whether Diane's actions or my lying was worse.

We had our group lunch Friday instead of Thursday because we had wanted to spend Thursday down in the cafeteria. We brought in clever sandwiches. We had croissants, lettuce wraps, pitas and brioche buns. We had lunch meat, cheeses, vegetables and some various types of chips. We looked absurd in our various costumes and with our hairy shoulders. Diane was eating a lettuce wrap with grilled chicken and I was eating a pita stuffed with pizza toppings. While the others were laughing about our spirit week, I asked Diane, "So did you make memes of your students?"

Diane smiled. "Oh yes. If a student asks me an annoying question, I take a picture of them and make it into a meme. The other day someone asked me in my sixth hour if they could take the test a different day because they had been absent the day before. So I made a meme of their picture. I mean, what were you going to do tonight that you couldn't have done the night before? He was on a field trip the day before too."

"I heard Donna talking to you about it," I admitted.

"Whatever," Diane chuckled. "I hope it blows up a bit because we're not moving towards one of us getting fired at a breakneck speed."

"She seemed pissed at me too," I said. "She was asking me suspicious questions about the spirit week and seemed highly annoyed at how easily I lied to her."

"Good," Diane concluded. "Maybe we'll be fired soon, although I hope I get to do my big idea before it happens."

"What shenanigans are you two plotting over there?" Josh interrupted us.

"Both of us got a bit of a scolding from Donna today," I announced.

"Ooh, someone's in trouble," Christine teased.

"Well one of you had better get fired soon," Darnell told us. "I'm not doing parent teacher conferences if you can't pull it off by the end of November."

"I've always wondered what it would be like to have wine at conferences," Emily pondered.

"I was thinking more along the lines of conferences with a megaphone," David offered. The idea of talking to parents through a megaphone caused a few of us to burst into laughter. Mary struggled to pull herself together for a few seconds.

"Your kid doesn't try very hard," Mary announced like she was holding a megaphone. She continued laughing.

"No, I can't make an appointment for you during conferences, you should have followed the instructions before just rudely showing up," Darnell spoke into his megaphone.

"You guys joke, but you know that Scott and I are showing up on Monday with megaphones for our teaching now," Diane announced. I smiled happily at the prospect of that one. Just then two teachers that weren't part of our group walked in and joined our lunch. Our conversation switched over to the funny costumes we had worn and seen all week and some complaining about kids whining.

On my way back from lunch I thought about how next week I really needed to ramp up my efforts. It was surprisingly difficult to accomplish a lot of pranks. They were hard to think of, they took a lot of time, and even teaching without grading was still a lot of work. The trampoline was still sitting in my classroom, and yet I don't think the principal was even aware. I couldn't move it into the hallway without disassembling the entire thing too because it didn't fit through the door. I came up with an idea for Monday though. I talked it over with my fourth hour as I ignored their repeated questions about why I had fish on my shoulders. I gave them instructions and then told them to discreetly spread the idea around to other trustworthy students on Monday morning. They were excited but I needed them to contain the idea enough that administration didn't find out prematurely.

Later that hour Diane walked into my room with a leash with a fake bear attached. The bear had a note that said, "Please do not feed me fish. I am training to help blind people." I laughed.

"Who's running practice today?" I asked after I appreciated her efforts with the bear.

"Let's both go," she said.

"Sounds good. I'm in no rush, and we've been slacking a bit as coaches the last three weeks," I agreed. We ended up running in two groups and doing a workout where we ran slow for a while and then fast for a bit and switched back and forth. It was a timed workout and Diane took the faster group. Then we did a mile on the track where we ran in our groups and the last person had to sprint to the front while we ran in a line. Our season only had about 3 weeks left, so whoever didn't get fired would stay on and make sure the students had a coach.

Chapter 16 Cattle

The week before had been a fun week, but this week I was ready to get fired. It was time to start pushing a bit more and to start doing more outlandish things that were noticed by the administration more. I felt like last week had finished with Donna ready to consider termination as an option finally, and I wanted to get that extra money. I was sure Diane was also going to be pushing hard as well. I had two ideas for Monday. The first was that early in the morning I came in and assembled a bunch of boxes. Then I carried them into the hallway near the front office, but where students would go during passing time. Then about four minutes before first hour ended, I left class and went and built a big giant box fort in the middle of the hallway to block everyone. When the bell rang the first few students could squeeze around the sides but soon the congestion started to cause students to throw boxes, climb over the structure and other creative solutions. It was a complete mess and the hallway ended up completely trashed.

Meanwhile, Diane had gone ahead with the megaphone. But instead of using it for teaching, she was insulting students in the hallway with it during passing. "Could you walk any slower? Are you trying to be late to class? In America we walk on the right side of the hallway." To make things more obnoxious, she would follow random students for an uncomfortably long period of time. When she caught two students kissing, things got ugly. "It is 8:34 in the morning. Did you have a cup of coffee before you felt the urge to make out in the hallway? Does it ruin the moment when I ask you questions about kissing while on a megaphone?" The students desperately tried to get away from her, but to their dismay, the megaphone carried for quite a distance.

At lunch, I ate with the crew and they looked at some of the fun things they were trying. I told them the goal is this week. They agreed that our contest had gone on long enough, and we should make a concerted effort, and that Diane would win if we didn't get it done this week. The growing sentiment was that Donna was considering disciplining one of us in the hopes that it would get the others to act right again. And we all thought she was close to the point where firing would be an option. But it would take the right mischief to get there. After lunch was where I hoped to stake my claim. When my fourth hour finally arrived, I told them to spread the word now in any way that they could. They pulled out their phones and sent messages and used social media. I had to negotiate the rest and Josh was my assistant.

Josh walked into the main office and told them he needed help with a student. He had brought a student with him that was having a fake seizure down the hall. While the staff ran out to deal with that, I snuck in the side door. I punched in the code to use the PA system. They probably thought they were about to hear something about help for the student in the hallway. Instead I let loose a big giant moo. "MOOOOOOOO." I snuck back out the side door and went the long way back to class. Along the way I heard it happening. I had gotten the idea from the father of one of my high school friends. From various classes I heard big loud "MOOOOOOs" happening. They grew in frequency and intensity. Then I heard the clattering of desks. The mooing was intense and mooing students burst into the hallways out of classes. They were slowly shifting their desks to move and they had formed giant clumps.

It was called a cattle drive. Once the moo had happened over the PA, multiple response moos had happened and then students had formed cattle herds while sitting in their desks. And nearly the whole school had picked up on it. Some herds had gone into the hallways to stampede around for a while. Others had formed one big mess of desks in their classes. Teachers had no idea what was going on. Except for Josh. Josh was just finishing up with his actor student, and they were heading back to class feeling much better when the stampedes happened. My whole class was mooing down the hallway while their desks scratched noisily along the floor.

As the "cows" made their way throughout the hallways, the administration had no idea what to do. They had students everywhere mooing. They had teachers clueless as to what had happened or how to bring their classes back to attention. Some teachers tried yelling but the event had taken most by surprise and they were confused about how to respond. Diane was in the hallway doing her best cowgirl impression with the megaphone. "Get back to class, none of you are actually cows. Except for maybe you, the smell makes it debatable."

I hoped that she wouldn't get the credit for the stampede, although I figured my voice was recognizable on the PA. Then all of a sudden, a large crashing sound happened. A student had tried to cattle drive down the stairs and he had fallen down the steps while in his desk. Another student screamed and lots of adults rushed towards the stairs. The other students slowly started moving back into their classrooms. They were trying to have haste, but the desks were hard to negotiate through the doors. The student who fell was struggling to get out from the desk but had landed in a way that made him stuck. He wasn't seriously hurt, but it had been a terrifying sound, and I was panicked. No one wanted a student to be hurt.

As we rushed towards him, the student assured us, "I'm fine, I'm not hurt. I'm sorry about the desk. I didn't mean to fall." I breathed for a second. Then Donna looked at me with a fury and exclaimed, "My office, NOW!" Then she turned to Diane. "You too!" Diane and I made our way back to the office. I figured this would be the moment. We both were thinking hard about our strategies to not give away our positions of wanting to be fired, but to be just obnoxious enough to get fired.

Maurice was with Donna, helping the student and getting the mess organized from the desk fracturing. Diane and I walked right into her office and sat down. "Do you think this is it?" I asked. I was pretty nervous although also hopeful.

"No, I think it's going to take more," Diane answered. "Do you have a plan for in here?"

"I've been thinking about this for a while, but this was not the scene that I thought would land me in here." We could hear someone coming. It was Donna. She closed the door, went straight to her desk and sat down.

"So listen," she started speaking in an exasperated tone. "I know I should probably be furious about what just happened. But I'm too busy to put my emotions in at the moment. The last time you two messed up the superintendent took notice and so this time things aren't going to go through me. I had talked with her earlier after I spoke to Scott. I thought you were clearly lying about not being involved in the spirit week. I thought Diane was clearly lying to me about the production of the memes. So before today's new incident took place the district administration agreed to conduct an investigation on both of you. They'll be meeting with you tomorrow. You are both going to be out of school the entire day and you will report to their office at 9am. You are recommended to bring your union representative with you, and if you wish to speak to them today, you can do that as well. Look, I love both of you, but lately you've been making the dumbest decisions and I don't understand why it has continued to this point. You should have been keeping a low profile, but instead I've got Scott mooing over the damn PA and Diane barking orders at students with a megaphone. And now a student nearly got badly hurt because of you two, and it's out of my hands. I hope you can get everything straightened out, but you're beyond my reach at this point. What questions do you have?"

I thought about asking where do babies come from, but at this point it seemed like it was out of Donna's hands anyways. "Are we going to be meeting together or just one of us at a time?" I asked.

"You'll both be there, but I'm sure they'll probably talk to you individually," Donna responded. You could tell that even after all of the stupid things we had done, she still had a soft spot for us.

"What should we do about cross-country practice today?" Diane asked.

"You can still run practice, just don't do anything stupid while you're there. If you want to cancel tomorrow I understand," Donna decided. Diane and I looked at each other trying to think of anything else we needed to ask. We both shrugged, got up and walked out. Donna was already dealing with something else before the door closed.

"Practice still today?" I asked.

"Yeah, one of us today and one of us tomorrow sounds good to me," Diane replied.

"I'd rather take today's practice if that's ok," I suggested. Diane nodded in agreement. The team and I did long slow run, and I thought about what tomorrow should entail. I called Josh on my way home, and he came over to meet with me and plan.

He arrived a few minutes after I did, even though I had stopped to pick up some dinner for us on the way. We ate outside on the deck so others couldn't hear us. I explained what had happened when we met with Donna.

"I can't believe a kid fell down the stairs in a desk," he said. "I'm glad he didn't get hurt, but man that helps both of you get close to getting fired."

I nodded. "Donna didn't even seem mad. It was like she was overwhelmed by the whole thing and couldn't invest her energy into it," I explained. "I think deep down she knows it doesn't all add up and so she's shut down a bit. I'm glad it's moved on beyond her, but I need to play tomorrow correctly. I've gotta choose the right outfit, say the right things, and if I can play my cards right and let loose a fart at an opportune time..."

Josh started laughing. "If you fart again and don't get fired..."

"Technically, she still might think it's a medical condition," I justified.

"I don't know what you should wear," Josh said thoughtfully. "I mean, you can't wear scrubs or they'll be thrown off, but you shouldn't dress too nicely either."

"I was thinking about wearing a nice shirt that has a sports logo on it," I offered up.

"But if they're a fan of that team, it looks like you're sucking up," Josh countered. "What if you wear something really nice but it's clearly women's clothing. Like a pants suit."

"How about a complete tuxedo?" I asked.

"Yes, that's it. Full tux is totally weird and hilarious. Especially if you fart."

"What should I do when they accuse me of all of the crazy things I've done?" I asked. "They'll probably look over my email, and it's possible they'll go into my room and find the full-size trampoline in there."

"I say you deny everything initially, ask a lot if that's all that they know about in suspicious tones, and then later threaten to sue a lot," Josh summarized.

"Or should I say that Diane said I could as an explanation for every weird thing I've done?"

"Don't blame her; we don't want her to get fired. You're this close to pulling this off so don't go screwing it up with bad strategy!" Josh said getting slightly fired up as he spoke.

"Should I do weird things like fidget, tap the floor with my foot or stare at people?"

"Yes, maybe you should do annoying things that students do like bottle flipping or ask to go to the bathroom a bunch of times," Josh recommended.

"What about going on the attack? Do we have any enemies from the district administrators?"

"If you get the one that sends out the stupid mass emails, I'm all for giving a piece of your mind about that," Josh admitted. "Even if it doesn't help our case, that's a message that needs to get sent."

"I think he left last year to another district," I said.

"Oh, well I linked his email to go directly to my trash, so I guess I missed the goodbye party," Josh said smirking. "What if you brought a fake petition to protest your firing and all of the signatures we make right now?" We continued coming up with stupid and vindictive ideas. We actually put together a fake petition that was incredibly stupid looking and clearly a phony. It was a blast, and I felt much more at ease. It was hard to transition out of feeling like I was in trouble and should be apologizing. But this helped me work out a character and a plan for tomorrow. I was feeling ready.

Chapter 17 Central Office

I woke up at the normal time because I was not going to tell my wife that I was going to try and get fired today. There was no point in freaking her out, although I hoped I could clue her in soon. Instead I met Diane for breakfast off of campus. I was dressed in a full tuxedo. Diane had worn leggings and a suggestive top. We looked absurd. Diane seemed pretty confident in her ability to swing this to her side, but I felt prepared as well. We left a generous tip and headed over to the district office. We brought four decaf coffees in to go cups with us.

When we got to the office it was about five minutes until 9am. We ended up waiting until about 9:25 before they finally called us in. I don't know if that was meant to be a power play, but it may have backfired because now I was even more intent on being destructive and aggressive. We walked in with cold decaf coffee. "Would anyone like a coffee?" I asked. Some of the administrators moved to take a coffee. "They're all decaf," I explained. The faces of a couple of the administrators dropped, and no one took a coffee. It was funny to me and probably should have been awkward. I left them out for the odor to fill the room and irritate some people as we talked.

I recognized the person in charge but did not know what his name was. I had just seen him before at a couple of school events. The superintendent was not present, but there were four total administrators. "It's hot in here," I commented loudly.

"Feel free to take off your jacket," the administrator said calmly.

"No thanks," I said with an inflection on thanks. Then I started fake coughing for about twelve seconds.

The administrator started introducing himself, "My name is Bob, and Will and I will be meeting with Diane; JD and Dolores will meet with Scott."

"Scott and I prefer to stay together," Diane announced.

Bob responded, "That's fine with us, whatever will make you more comfortable." He then led us into a conference room with really nice furniture. I was displeased that they got nice furniture but we had such lousy supplies and funding for supplies. I made a note in my notebook about it.

As we sat down, I set down all four coffees on the table. I didn't even drink coffee, so it was even funnier to me to buy four decaf coffees at 9am just so people wouldn't have coffee. Dolores started things off by saying, "Well, I am one of the legal representatives for the district. I've been reviewing what has taken place for both of you, and I must say that I'm struggling to understand. Is it true that Scott you dove under a desk and then later farted in front of the superintendent?"

"I don't remember exactly what happened. Am I supposed to put my hand on a Bible or something here?" I asked in an exasperated voice.

"No, you're not on trial, we're just investigating some incidents that have been brought to our attention," Bob explained.

"Well it feels like you're trying to call me stupid," I articulated. "And I will gladly demonstrate my intelligence right now." I pulled out a whiteboard and started explaining how to predict reaction spontaneity based on Gibbs free energy.

"Mr. Miles, that's really not necessary," Dolores interrupted. "Please put your whiteboard away. It should not be needed."

I hesitated, looked around at everyone in the room. Then I set the whiteboard off to the side, but still on the table like I was very suspicious that someone would take it.

Dolores turned to Diane and said, "Mrs. Bird, is it true that you have a wheel in your class that students spin and then it makes fun of them."

Diane thought hard like she was confused and spoke very slowly. "I mean, we have a wheel. I wouldn't call it my classroom as much as it is our classroom, and it definitely doesn't make fun of students. It just points out their deficiencies in a comedic manner."

"But one of the results is 'you smell so bad that your parents apologize in advance to your teachers,' is that correct?" Dolores asked.

"Yes, that's a good one," Diane responded cheerfully. "Actually though, I think it says 'Your parents emailed your teachers to say they don't like you and aren't proud of you' or something like that."

"Does another section say 'Nobody likes you and you have no friends?'" Dolores asked.

"I can't remember every section of it, but there are other ones that students helped design that might be something like that," Diane admitted casually.

"Ok, that's fine for now," Dolores said while writing some notes. "Scott, is it true that you currently have a trampoline in your classroom and that students use it?"

"Yes, that is correct," I spoke like there was a microphone in front of me and I was at a press conference.

"Can you talk about what educational value the trampoline has?" she pushed.

"Yes. Originally, I had put up the trampoline, using my own money for the record, in order to help students sit with ergonomic posture. It turns out though that the trampoline connected to many chemistry lessons on stability, physical chemistry, material science engineering and bonding. It also was fun, and I made sure to remove any unsafe materials from its proximity."

"But isn't the trampoline full sized? Were there issues with the location and students' heads bumping into the ceiling?" Bob asked.

"I mean, it was a trampoline, I'd say about yay big," I responded and stood up holding my hands outstretched while spinning to show how big it was. "No one bumped any heads because I made sure that they didn't do that."

237

"Did you also light fireworks with students present?" Dolores followed up.

"Yes, but I was trained in order to do so safely."

"What was the extent of your training?" Bob jumped in.

I paused. "Well, my friend is a professional, and he trained me."

"What did the training involve? How long was it? Do you have any official certification?" Dolores asked persistently.

"Well I called him and he walked me through everything and how to not screw it up. But I also made sure that the students were far away that they wouldn't be in danger even if something went wrong. I also only did fireworks inside at the end of the hour to limit inhalation."

"You did fireworks indoors?" Dolores asked incredulously. "What were you thinking?"

"It's called teaching," I said while pretending to be offended. "What would you have done? Used methanol and lit a bunch of front row students on fire? I was teaching students how light can identify chemicals and how light is produced and how chemical reactions cause acceleration of electrons." I motioned to Diane.

"I mean yeah, it's not 1960 or whenever you went to school. We do actual science," Diane backed me up while slipping in a completely unnecessary insult about their age. Bob and Dolores looked at each other, leaned in and whispered and then faced back towards us.

"Diane, can you explain what the rationale was for bringing in a peacock to school?" Dolores asked.

"Which one?" Diane responded and then continued on saying, "I'm just kidding. I only have one peacock. That was a peacock from my farmer friend, and he was trying to raise the peacock as a guide bird for those that struggle with visual impairments. So the bird would help people, but I'm not sure if this district cares about those with impairments or if they just think they should live separate from everyone else." Diane was the perfect balance of accusation, nonsense and judgement.

"Is that true?" I asked Dolores.

"Is what true?" she responded. Instead of repeating myself, I started writing furiously in my notebook, then turned the page dramatically with my eyebrows raised high.

"Diane, I have three emails this month where you replied all to the staff where the email only said 'ok' and nothing else. Why did you persist in sending those?" Dolores asked.

"What should I have said?" Diane questioned back.

"Many of the emails don't warrant a reply," Dolores explained.

"Ok...." Diane said while looking confused and mildly annoyed.

"Scott, how did the students know that you were going to say moo over the PA and then how did so many students know to pretend to be a cow?" Bob asked.

"I honestly have no idea. I mean I had told them the story about the cattle drive when my friend's dad had been in school but that was a while ago. And I didn't moo on purpose. I just had picked up the PA and it somehow had turned on and that's when I accidentally mooed." I stressed the word accidentally.

"You accidentally dialed in the code?" Dolores asked.

"I must have," I admitted.

"It's a six-digit code," Bob said suspiciously.

"Wow," I responded. "That was some coincidence. Maybe someone had put part of the code in earlier because I don't think I hit many buttons or maybe not any at all."

"Diane, can you explain why you had a megaphone with you during the cattle drive?" Dolores asked.

"It makes my voice louder," Diane said. Everyone waited for her to explain more but she just sat there. I felt like laughing, but I took a breath and kept it in.

"Super," Dolores finally muttered and wrote something down. They were both visibly annoyed. The other two people had just sat there and taken some notes sporadically.

"Diane, can you talk about the decision to have this poster frame in your room?" Delores pulled out a photo of Diane's poster that said "Students that are currently annoying me" and put it in front of her.

"Yes," Diane said and then paused to collect her thoughts. "This was because we had a lot of below average behaviors in some classes, and I knew that would not suffice, so this was a motivational tool for those students. I have data that shows that it worked."

"What do you mean you have data?" Bob asked.

"I took data on how many below average behaviors I had before and after," Diane explained. "Before I had a lot, and after I started the poster, I redefined the word average and then I had way fewer incidents."

"How can you have the number of below average incidents change? Wouldn't there always be the same amount of below average incidents?" Bob asked curiously.

"Thank you!" I said vigorously. Everyone looked around curiously like they had no idea why I was annoyed. "Are you not aware of the district trying to decrease the number of below average students?"

"Relative to their peers?" Bob asked incredulously. Dolores quickly leaned over and whispered something to him. He nodded and started to move on. "Tell me more about what fireworks you were using for educational purposes."

"Hang on, what did you just whisper to him?" I redirected.

"Nothing," Dolores quickly muttered.

"Why would you lie to me?" I said with a raised voice. "You clearly just whispered something to him. What was it?"

"You will not speak to me like that," Dolores started to become unhinged a little bit.

I turned towards the two people who hadn't spoken yet. "What are the consequences for her lying to me directly in this deposition?"

JD responded, "This isn't a deposition, and she's not the one this disciplinary hearing is for."

"We'll see how that changes. I will be informing everyone about what just happened," Diane jumped on my side.

"Will you also be explaining to everyone how you dragged a turtle around the school with a fake note about how the turtle was being trained to help blind people?" JD casually tossed back. "Will you be explaining how you inhumanely used the turtle for physics experiments?"

"We're getting off task," Bob said trying to calm the room. "Scott, tell us about the Jesus chemistry video."

"What about it?" I asked.

"What was your thought process on making the video?" He responded.

"I made a chemistry video where I was dressed up as White Jesus. It was engaging and creative and respectfully done. The students learned a lot, and it went well."

"What about your students that aren't Christian?" Dolores asked.

"I'm no religion expert, but I believe that Jesus is not limited to the Christian religion. A lot of religions and secular historians are aware of Jesus, but disagree on his exact role. Do you have a problem with Jesus?"

No one answered and the Will lawyer person whispered something to JD, and they both wrote in their notebooks.

"Diane, can you explain the process for how you had students vote on how stupid other student's test answers were?"

"Well, I would put an answer up and we all reflected on the accuracy. I wouldn't refer to an answer as stupid. But instead, we would look at what process might have led to the mistake."

"One of your students says that not only were the names posted along with the response, but that you made the student stand up and read their answer to the class," Bob read from his report. "It also says that one answer you said was the worst thing that you had ever read, and you wished that you had been hit by a bus instead of reading that answer."

"I mean, I guess if we're just going to take students at their exact word," Diane redirected. "What was the grade of the student interviewed? A lot of students will say anything for a chance to move up unfortunately. Especially now with the emphasis on being above average."

"That's true," I offered in agreement. "If you interviewed students, probably they mostly lied. Kind of like Dolores did earlier if you forgot when she lied to me."

Dolores rolled her eyes slightly and then turned to Diane, "Is it true that you said to a student that their

243

answer was so stupid that their middle school teacher should get suspended?" Diane just shrugged and stared impatiently at the wall.

"I agree with Diane," I said. "What's the point of this meeting? To fling wild accusations of anything you could convince a student to say? What do you want us to say about these stories that have little supporting evidence?"

"We have photographic evidence for many of them," Dolores explained. "I mean I can go show you the trampoline in your room right now or the poster where you ranked the bottom ten students. Most of these accusations have several credible witnesses and you've admitted to most of the offenses listed."

"Well, what is the point of this meeting then if everything has been decided?" I pushed.

"We're trying to listen to your side of the story and also evaluate what the appropriate disciplinary process is," Bob answered.

"Well, it doesn't feel like it," Diane responded.

"Well, this isn't a typical rundown of offenses," Dolores stated. "You made a fake announcement for a big butts club that would be fictitiously run by the assistant principal. Both of you appear to have called in for a sub multiple times while you were at school so that you could hang out while they supervised your classes. Both of you were highly disruptive at the district PD presentation. Scott has a trampoline in his class. Diane has been having students run races at full sprint while blindfolded. Several students were injured and one got a concussion. I'm sorry but I don't know how to ask you in a serious tone about all of these offenses. This is the most insane list of teacher violations that anyone has ever seen. The emails you've both sent to parents are incredibly insulting. One of them says "LOL, nope!" and nothing else. Do you even know which one of you sent that email?"

"Was the lol capitalized or lowercase?" I asked. Dolores looked like she was going to snap her pencil. She stood up and walked out of the room to take a break.

Bob continued while she was gone. "This is a very unusual set of violations. I also don't really know how to ask about them because they individually seem absurd and the sheer number of violations is unprecedented. It seems to be contagious too. We got a report yesterday that a teacher was dipping their hands in syrup before passing back students' papers. I guess we're looking for an explanation as to how you can do so much wrong in such a short period of time. Neither of you has any discipline action in over thirty years of combined teaching, but this past month have had a file that is bigger than a chemistry textbook. What do you two have to say about all of this?" Dolores walked back in and sat down.

Diane started. "I guess this looks bad, but individually most of these actions were either funny, or engaging or in response to something that students needed. I feel like we're over-reacting, and I think this meeting is a little much. I mean what if the teacher with syrup hands had a medical condition?"

"I think there are some disconnects between good science teaching methods. It's different in other classes because you aren't at the intellectual level of a chemistry class. In chemistry or physics, you're doing complex thinking that involves reading, mathematics, science all at the same time. So I get that you find some of these methods extreme, but we're just matching the energy of the material. I mean, did any student complain about anything we did?"

"Yes, we have a large number of student and parent complaints," Bob affirmed.

"That's social media for you," Diane explained. "One parent complains and the rest smell blood in the water. They think it will boost their grades to exaggerate and put pressure on us to comply."

Dolores stood up and started pacing around and looked incredibly upset. I hadn't even noticed when she had returned because I was focusing on not laughing anytime Diane spoke. "Why don't we take a break for a bit," Bob instructed. If you two would like to go get some lunch we can meet back here in an hour."

***

We agreed, and Diane and I headed out for lunch. "That was hilarious. What do you think she whispered to him about the below average initiative?" I asked.

"I'm sure she was explaining what incompetent individual came up with it that they are now colluding together to cover up," Diane theorized.

"Do you think they'll fire us? What if we both get fired at the same time?"

"I'd bet that if we both go down, that we'd split the money evenly for all eight of us," Diane guessed. "And that works for me. Either way, we're going to have more than enough for the rest of our lives."

"I'm trying to think of the best way to handle this meeting, but I wonder if instead I should be digging for more dirt," I said.

"I think at least one of us is done today, so it's probably time to let go of our roles here," said Diane. "Let's go enjoy one last meal together as employees and hope we can celebrate with our families after lunch."

We went out and grabbed some subs. We reminisced about what the school was like when I started and who else we wished would have been involved. We had one English teacher back in the day that was intense, and she would have really gone after this competition. She used to make comments like we did without the incentive. Then we thought through if we could have had one student this year instead of the year we had them originally. Diane had one student about 18 years ago that had been awful. Incredibly rude and inappropriate and constantly insubordinate. We had fun thinking of what we could have done if that had been this year. Finally, we refilled our drinks and headed back to the office. It was time to find out if we were being fired or if we'd have to submit to some more questioning.

The four people were all there, and now the superintendent and another person that we didn't recognize was there. We sat down quietly. At the beginning we were prepared to fight back and make things awkward, but now we were both ready to accept our fate, and I think both of us were ready to reveal our secret once one of us was fired.

The superintendent greeted us, "Hello Scott, hello Diane. How are both of you?"

"I'm good, how is your day going?" I responded cheerfully. I felt pretty good here at the end of the trip.

"I'm doing well also," Diane chimed in.

"Great," she responded. "I've talked things over with Bob and Dolores about the investigation. We've decided that many of the actions taken were odd, offensive, extreme and destructive to the environment here. We take these issues very seriously. So unfortunately, I regret to inform you that you will both be issued a third disciplinary letter in your file. You will both be suspended for one day with pay and you will both be placed on probation upon return. You will have to be observed daily for one week and then after that you will be observed once more per month through the school year. I hope you take the rest of today to think over what you are working towards and can re-establish yourselves as the teachers I heard about prior to this month."

Diane and I were shocked. It was a complete non-punishment. We hadn't even been apologetic during the interrogation. We had made up a bunch of counter accusations and been dismissive. They were suspending us for today, the day that we were already out. So that was nothing. And probation would be annoying normally, but that's nothing but a bunch of work for Donna or Eric. They weren't going to fire us ever at this rate.

Dolores started explaining further, "You can challenge this through the union but if you do it will mean that your suspension will be served at a later date. If you have any questions you can ask us now." Dolores had a huge smile on her face.

"I'm sorry, I'm going to need a minute here," I said and I left the room. Diane followed behind me. "I don't think they're going to fire us ever," I whispered to her. "We could not have treated that meeting any more disrespectfully and still nothing."

"I'm surprised, but I still think we can pull it off," Diane answered. "We're both on probation now with a daily observation. I say we keep going and make sure we get this done this week." Reluctantly I eventually agreed. We went back into the room and nearly everyone had left. Will had some papers for us to sign and instructions on what we could and could not do along with a copy of our disciplinary letters. Even though they were disappointing in that they weren't termination letters, they would definitely be a prized possession if we ever got to the end of this contest. We asked Will for a copy for each and after he made them we left the meeting and went home to plan.

We were off for the day, but figured our suspension was tomorrow so we should be ok to pop in to the school for a few minutes. Diane drove and I sat in disbelief. "I can't believe they gave us another wimpy punishment," I exclaimed in frustration. "We could not have been more ridiculous and they knew everything that we had done. They even searched our emails!"

Diane paused before speaking. "Well, obviously I'm slightly disappointed that it didn't happen, but that meeting was gold. You were hilarious in there." I agreed completely that the exchanges were overwhelmingly funny. I texted the other six to meet us in my classroom. It was during my prep hour so it should be empty. We entered the school through a side door so that we weren't noticed by Donna. When we got to my room there were four teachers in there already. Darnell, David, Christine and Josh were all sitting around waiting for us to announce who had been fired. Diane ran to get Mary and I went to get Emily but Emily was walking down the hallway towards me.

"So, who got fired?" Darnell wanted to know.

"Nobody got fired," I admitted. There was an obvious look of impatience and disappointment in the room. While this was fun, it had gone for a bit now and there was a lot of money on the line.

"Did you beg to keep your jobs?" David asked. He asked politely but subtle frustration was evident in the tone. He was wearing a striped shirt with a striped tie that didn't quite match.

"Look, I know this is getting to a point where we'd like to be wrapping things up," Diane expressed. "But we were absolute snobs in that meeting, they had a list of everything both of us had done and they still didn't fire us. We are suspended for one day, on probation with weekly observations and have received another letter in our file."

"That's it?" Christine asked incredulously.

"Wow," Mary mumbled. "I thought they would have at least put in a suspension for a few days while they interviewed your students or something." Mary was wearing a shirt that bragged about her weight loss and showed her standing on the moon.

Emily had been waiting to speak and finally found a moment to interject. "Look, this has been great, but I think it's time to think of an alternative way to settle this. We've been having a great time, but I feel that in the next month this will turn ugly. It won't be enjoyable and we don't need it to go there. What else can we do?"

Mary confidently responded, "I think you're right, but we're not there yet. I'm confident we'll be taking home the prize and soon. I know it's frustrating that the district is soft, but they don't have a wealth of applicants to replace us."

"Should we open the rules a bit more and allow some insubordination?" Josh asked genuinely.

"No," I responded. "We should plug along with what we're doing. It's working, just slower than we'd hope. Let's give it some more time. Today feels like a setback, let's take a day to cool off and if nothing

251

progresses in a week, we can have a meeting where we talk about alternatives."

Then Diane and I recounted the entire meeting for everyone. The mood settled a little bit as we acted out Dolores, Will and the others questioning us. Soon laughter filled the room, and we postulated about who they were covering up for about the below average debacle. Finally, everyone went back to their classrooms. It was just Diane and I and the sub had returned to teach the last hour of the day. Diane and I were getting ready to drive back to pick up my car and head home. Right before the bell rang Amy Well walked by. "Hey Mr. Miles, can I talk to you a bit or are you in a meeting right now?" she asked.

Diane said, "I'll hang out in Mary's room, come get me when you're ready."

As Diane walked away, I turned towards Amy and asked, "So what's up?"

Amy seemed nervous. "Well I heard from some people that you were in trouble today. I mean, I know you've done some weird stuff in class lately and I was just worried. Some kids had started a rumor that you had been fired."

I had to think for a second on how to respond. "I did have a meeting today, I have not been fired," I finally said. I wasn't sure what to add to that.

Amy looked relieved. "Ok, I'm sorry I brought this up, I know it's weird. I was just, well chemistry is really hard for me to learn, but I feel like I'm starting to understand everything and I was worried if you left that I'd start to struggle again. If you need someone to talk on your behalf, I'd be happy to. My mom also said she would. Sorry if she emails you too much. She's a bit of a mess because my older sister fell apart in high school and she takes all of her worrying out on my teachers."

Amy headed to her next class and I was alone with my thoughts. What a lovely set of compliments and while I had had issues with Mrs. Well I found it nice that she was willing to speak on my behalf. I also felt a little bad that soon I would be abandoning Amy and my other students. I took a deep breath and walked over to Mary's room to grab Diane. We drove back together mostly in silence.

Chapter 18 The Return

It was the week before school started. All eight of us had returned to Michigan to meet up to celebrate. Some came from far away, but Josh and I were still local. We rented out a room at The Teacher's Lounge bar. Diane had paid in advance for us to have an open bar all night. Josh and I arrived first. We both still saw each other regularly. Diane arrived next. She had moved out of state and had been traveling internationally. I believe one of her trips had been with Darnell's family.

"You know, I could have paid for this since I'm still working," I greeted her.

"I took it out of my bonus winnings," she replied while smiling.

"Had to rub that in, didn't you," Josh smirked. "I thought we had it won too."

Mary and Emily got there at the same time. Mary hadn't seen Diane for a while so they immediately started catching up. Emily chatted with us and Christine walked in slightly into our conversation. Darnell and David rode in together from the same hotel. All eight of us were back together for the first time since shortly after Diane had been fired.

"Anyone bring any emails to respond to?" Darnell announced as he and David walked in. We all laughed, thinking back to the fun we had when we were aiming to get fired. We reminisced about the whole thing. From the meeting in Josh's room, to the contest, to the days after Diane had been fired.

"I thought they weren't going to fire us unless one of us escalated it to the point where we'd violate the contest rules," I said. "That meeting before the end was so bad, and they still gave us a slap on the wrist."

"Good thing team Diane had a plan for right after the meeting," David added.

"More like our plan was finally ready to enact," Mary corrected him. "We worked on that thing for two weeks to get everything ready."

"So did you two work today?" Mary asked Josh and myself.

"No, we have a lot of arrangements worked out, and we don't go in whenever we don't want to basically," Josh explained. We both had continued teaching in spite of our financial situations. "The biggest thing is that we both use our salary to pay to have a teaching assistant. They've been working with some local universities to supply us with student teachers that get paid a stipend and part of their tuition. Then they do all of the parts of teaching we don't want to do. They teach first hour when we want to sleep in, they do all of the PD, they do all of the grading."

"And they respond to emails and conference requests," I added. "We basically just do the fun parts of teaching and it's amazing. The district was pretty easy to negotiate with because they had six teachers leaving, and we would have made it eight vacancies. Even with the extra money, it would have been rough hiring eight teachers mid-year."

"Did they get people hired?" Darnell asked.

"The money we donated to give out signing bonuses helped," I explained. "But there just aren't that many candidates. We got some hired quickly, a few later and the rest over the summer. They had to cover some classes with long term subs, but they used part of the bonus money to get those, so they made it work pretty well considering."

"When I talked to Donna about it, she was pretty forgiving," Josh added. "She was happy with her personal bonus we all chipped in for, and she was really happy that we had at least made rules to prevent things from going into the illegal zone."

"She loves the fund we started for weekly thousand dollar bonuses for staff," I told everyone. Everybody smiled. "Every week she talks about a staff member that has done a great job and she writes up a letter that she sends out to the entire school. The staff are mostly happy but there are a few that would get upset even if they won."

"I bet I know who one of those is," Mary interjected.

"Whatever," Josh said. "Some people don't want to be happy."

"How's Donna?" David asked.

"She's good," I replied. "Maurice also was much appreciative of his bonus, and he's still running the show for the most part. Donna has recovered nicely from our contest and seems to be pretty understanding and also happy that Josh and I are still working. I think having our money supply for desperate times also reduces some of her stress."

"So what are you two doing then?" Emily asked.

Josh started explaining his current work settings. "I come in later every day and they put my prep hour first, and second hour gets covered for me. I come in around 9am and teach two math preps. I do one harder one and one that's a bit easier, so I still get a mix of students. I don't do any grading, and my assistant handles everything else. She'll do that for the next two years and she earns enough from me to get her tuition paid and some savings money."

"I have someone for this year who runs everything," I said. "She'll graduate this year and if she doesn't find a job, she'll keep working for me until they do. She loves it because she makes a great salary, learns a lot and doesn't have too much to do because I run all of the classroom things that I want to. I teach chemistry all day, and I resigned from cross-country, but I still help with practice so that I'm free to do other things if I want. Our schedules are both incredibly flexible, and we still eat lunch together. There are a couple of new teachers that we've added to our lunch club, and they constantly joke that we should start a lottery club."

"Anyone we know?" Diane asked with a hint of jealousy.

"Mike, who teaches physical education, and then a new teacher named Amanda who teaches physics," Josh stated. Diane feigned jealousy.

"Sometimes the new bio teacher joins us too, but she's busy a lot of the time. So what are you six up to?" I asked.

"I have travelled everywhere," Darnell told us excitedly. "Every continent but Antarctica, and I think eighteen countries total just this year."

"Favorite so far?" Mary prodded.

"Probably Indonesia, but all of them have been amazing," Darnell admitted.

"I have also been traveling and one of our trips was with Darnell to China," Diane told us.

"I opened up a restaurant for fun. I have a lot of people help run it, so it's not too much work, but it's something I enjoy doing," Mary added.

"I've eaten at Mary's restaurant," David stated. "It was ok." David was wearing a blue button-down shirt with a classy pink tie.

"Whatever," Mary exclaimed. "You're just not high class enough to appreciate the stylings of food ambiance we deliver."

"I started writing a book about traveling through Central America," Emily announced. "It's not even close to done, but I've done a lot of the travel components."

"That sounds awesome," Christine replied. "Is it fiction or nonfiction?"

"Fiction," Emily answered. "But there's some historical context that's real as well."

We sat down and ordered some food and some drinks. I got a brownie sundae since it was a celebration. We talked more about travelling. What everyone missed from teaching. The other six had lots of suggestions of funny things that Josh and I could do now that we didn't need to teach. We talked about our new homes, showed each other pictures, talked about our new lives and what we missed and what we didn't. Diane finally told us, "I'm really glad that both of you are still teaching."

"We always joke that we wouldn't be if Scott had been the one to get fired," Josh said.

"I thought we were both going down in that meeting, and then they just completely blew everything off," I remembered.

"When we walked out you sounded like you wanted to quit the whole contest," Diane recalled. "But I knew I had one more big ticket item on the way."

"Your statue is still there," I announced. "It turns out that it is absurdly expensive to remove it and most of us still think it's hilarious." What had happened was that the weekend after our meeting Diane had brought a construction crew to build a structure that housed a statue of her. They poured cement and put in her plaque and statue. The statue was her holding a trophy in the shape of an apple. The plaque read "Diane Bird Best Teacher Ever Award." Around the trophy were a built-in set of lights so that in the mornings when it was still dark on our way to school, we got to see Diane's statue illuminated from afar.

"I was dying when I walked into school that Monday and saw you made a statue celebrating yourself," Josh recalled. "That was genius."

259

"They were so mad," Diane reminisced. "I had to meet with about eight administrators that day. I kept insisting that they not ruin my day and talked about how hard I had worked to finally win an award. They kept telling me that it was made up, and I insisted it was real. I even tried fake crying but they were not having it!"

"I still think it was the fact that you had tapped into their electrical system and poured cement that got them to fire you," David said. "If you had just dumped the statue, they would have tossed it in the garbage and not worried about it at all. But they couldn't remove it and didn't have the funds to hire someone."

"It made them feel helpless and so they broke," Darnell added.

"I loved that you threw yourself a congratulations breakfast for it," Emily said while laughing. "It was a damn good breakfast too!"

"Do you remember the announcement video?" Christine asked.

"Diane slicing off the head of the "2nd best teacher ever" with a laser sword, who could forget that?" I said.

"When they were about to fire me," Diane explained, "one of the administrators threatened to carve the word "Not" into the plaque. So it would say 'Not the best teacher ever award' instead. I busted out laughing. What an idiot."

"I bet that's the one!" Josh yelled. "That was probably the below average brainchild!"

"Yes!" Diane realized suddenly. "When he said that, the lady from our meeting eye rolled really hard."

"Dolores?" I asked. Diane nodded.

"Your statue is legendary," Josh said. "We always come up with other statues to put next to it."

"My favorite idea is to put up a statue that says 'This is Scott Miles, he's ok at teaching' and have it just be a statue of me while shrugging," I said.

"What about 'please stop talking to me, I'm a statue not a therapist?'" wondered Emily.

"Hah!" I laughed. "Our laminated signs are still up in a few spots."

"Is there going to be a spirit week this year?" David asked. "If so, we should all show up for cone day again."

"Maybe we'll do fake cast day and everyone can pretend to have broken limbs," Darnell quickly proposed as if he had been thinking about it since spirit week.

"David, do you remember that you used to walk like a weirdo down the hall all of the time back when we first taught so that if anyone was watching the cameras, they'd see you being stupid?" I asked.

"I kept doing that the entire time I taught there, including during the contest. Sometimes I'd pretend to pick my nose too," he admitted.

"Pretend," Diane stated using air quotes. "Scott and Josh, you can walk for the cameras now too."

I smiled as we came up with more dumb ideas. "I've missed all of you," I announced. "I'm really glad that we did that stupid contest, and it was the most fun I've had in my life. Even though I ended up not walking away from teaching and even though I only do the fun parts of it now, those weeks were the best."

Diane raised her glass for a toast. "Scott's right for once. Let's make sure that we keep meeting every once in a while. We have the finances to make sure it happens. But I also would like to take a moment to appreciate the most fun any of us will ever have had." Our glasses clinked and we all remembered the finer moments of our contest and our friendships. We stayed for quite a while that night. We caught up, but we spent most of the time joking about the past. We reminisced about the contest, the pranks, the reactions of other people. But we also talked about our teaching jobs before we had won the lottery. Back when we were just regular teachers eating lunch together and complaining about the bad things and enjoying the good ones. We had lived a lot of our lives together, and just like Josh and I weren't ready to remove ourselves from the investments we had made as teachers, none of us were ready to move on from our friendships.

"Look what I brought," Mary announced near the end of the night. She and Christina had purchased yearbooks for all of us. Each one came with signatures and notes from our students and from other staff. Donna and Maurice and a lot of our other friends had filled out notes for us. We passed them around and wrote each other notes. We looked at the pictures of our school. We laughed, we smiled and we were happy. The yearbooks reminded me that I had brought copies of my journal. I ran back to my car to show everyone the records I had kept. As we went through, we discovered that Josh had been the one to dip his hands in syrup before passing back papers.

After our night together, we made plans to meet again at the start of the school year next year. Josh and I weren't sure that we'd still be teaching then, but we planned on it tentatively. We met again the next day for lunch, but Christine and Darnell had already flown back to their new homes. As the week progressed, we dwindled until it was just Josh, Diane and me. Diane stopped by one of the cross-country practices to talk to the team. She knew quite a few of the runners still, and they had a lot of questions for her about her statue and the rest that had happened. Diane and I ran with the team. We both ran together and Diane was definitely a step slower than she had been the year before. That night was her last before she flew home, so we went back out one more time after practice.

We went back to the same bar we had gone to after we had put up the laminated signs all over the building. I remembered the emotions I had felt while thinking about not teaching anymore and what the transition would look like. "Do you remember when we came here after putting up signs that day?" Diane asked.

"I was just thinking about it," I admitted.

"I was having a hard time that night. What was it going to mean to not be a physics teacher anymore? I know I did other things, but it was a huge part of my identity; it still is. I still teach physics when I get the chance. I miss having my classroom now. I'm not at a point where I would actually start teaching again, but it really makes me happy that you and Josh stuck with it. It makes me feel like that part of me is still there and that I haven't completely left."

"I don't think I could do it if Josh didn't," I confessed. "It spreads the weirdness around just enough that I can still feel slightly normal. Even with all of the arrangements, it still comes to a point sometimes. Like one day I had a class that just would not shut up. And I remember thinking I don't need this, you know. I could just walk out at any point. But the good parts make that worth it. And I love those good parts. And I'm still not ready for those to be gone."

Diane nodded silently. I think we had a lot of similar struggles but Diane had been teaching for longer which made it harder to stay and harder to leave. "They haven't completely left me," she admitted.

"Does this mean you're coming in to teach one of my classes next week?" I asked. "Substitute Bird?"

"I like the sound of that," Diane pondered. "Diane Bird, best substitute ever..."

I laughed. I could picture the statue now. "Do you really think you could come in for a day?" I asked.

"No, I need a break. Maybe sometime down the road I'll dip my toe back in," Diane decided as she spoke. "I miss it, but I did this for a long time and the break has its perks too. But I need you to hear me, that I'm glad you two are still here. You keep teaching, not forever, but you make sure that when you leave that you feel confident about your statue that you'll put next to mine for second best teacher ever."

"I'll add it to my goal for the year," I stated plainly. Then I winked. Diane laughed.

Acknowledgements

Dave Fleming was my inspiration to write this book and without his thorough editing the writing would have been disgraceful. He and the rest of the B Pod Squad provided relentless opportunity to critically reflect on the many hijinks that could lead to a hilarious firing from the profession.

My mom and dad were both big influences for me to become a teacher. My mom has taught middle school English for nearly my entire life. One of my most frequent encounters growing up was to enter a room to find both of them reading books together.

My wife Hillary, also a teacher, is my everything. Without her help this never would have happened. Thank you also to my kids Emily and David for watching way too much tv so that I could have time to write.

And of course, thank you to all teachers. Teaching is a strenuous and awesome job. Too many teachers have helped me improve my own teaching to name, but know that your impacts are appreciated.

66473650R00163